THE DIVINER
is part of the
Classic Irish Fiction Series
edited by Peter Fallon
and published by
The O'Brien Press Dublin
and
Allison & Busby London

Also by Brian Friel

Brian Friel

THE DIVINER

The best stories of Brian Friel

with an introduction by

Seamus Deane

The O'Brien Press Dublin
Allison & Busby London

FIRST PUBLISHED 1983 BY THE O'BRIEN PRESS LTD
20 VICTORIA ROAD DUBLIN 6 IRELAND
AND ALLISON & BUSBY LTD
6A NOEL STREET, LONDON W1V 3RB
ORIGINALLY PUBLISHED AS *SELECTED STORIES* 1979
BY PETER FALLON'S GALLERY PRESS.

INTRODUCTION: SEAMUS DEANE 1979, 1982

BRITISH LIBRARY CATALOGUING IN PUBLICATION DATA
FRIEL, BRIAN
THE DIVINER.—(CLASSIC IRISH FICTION, ISSN 0332-1347; 2)
I. TITLE   II. SERIES
823'.914 [F] PR6056.R/

ISBN 0-86278-021-7 O'Brien Press
ISBN 0-85031-495-X Allison & Busby

PUBLISHED WITH THE ASSISTANCE OF
THE ARTS COUNCIL (AN CHOMHAIRLE EALAÍON)

BOOK DESIGN: MICHAEL O'BRIEN
TYPESETTING: CAHILL PRINTERS LTD.
PRINTED IN THE REPUBLIC OF IRELAND

CONTENTS

for Tom Kilroy

Introduction

If a story takes its form from the author's desire, it also gives form to the desire of its reader. The reader of this selection of Brian Friel's stories will find his desire moulded into form by the pressure of that local, intimate detail which emerges out of the author's knowledge of his society's moral code. Each story is social in its setting, moral in its implication. Time and again we have the impression that the small-town or village society, no matter how sharply it may be observed in its conformity to the powers of Church or class, has a moral code that belongs elsewhere. The narrowness of the social life is bitter, but the complexity of the moral life within is generous. Yet Brian Friel does not counterpose the two for the sake of contrast. Instead, he illustrates their interdependence, eliciting from us the recognition that the formal structures of social life are what we live by, not what we live for. Yet what we live for is clarified only by the insufficiency of what we live by. This may be no more than glimpsed in these stories; it receives a more sustained and indeed harsher treatment in the author's plays. But the co-existence of two realms, one clearly etched and social, the other amorphous and imaginative, which constitute together the one and the only world is insistently asserted. The separation of these realms, often threatened by sudden disaster, farce or illumination, is never permitted in the stories. In the plays, especially the more recent, it is enforced. But here, the author's insistence on the actuality of event and on the reality of imagination is quite impartial. His linguistic diplomacy is directed towards gaining recognition for both sides. This must be conceded by the reader when it is achieved by the writer.

The concession can only be willingly made when the language has a suasion that disguises its coercive aim, when the modesty of tone and approach is such that we feel persuaded we have discovered what we have just been shown. The syntax and vocabulary of these stories present no apparent problems. Brian Friel is, technically speaking, a traditional writer. The dislocations and the nuanced egoism of many modern texts are sternly avoided, even rejected, here. Yet each paragraph has the tension of writing that demands unremitting care from the reader. Nothing wilful, nothing willed, the workaday words, only slightly coloured by figure or weighted by pronounced rhythm, manage to be so informative, so quickly and easily blended into a narrative medium that we are at first aware only of the story, not the teller. Take, for example, the following passage from the opening paragraph of *The Widowhood System*:

> The very day his mother was buried, Harry Quinn set about converting the two attic rooms, from which she had ruled the house for the last nineteen years of her impossible dotage, into a model pigeon loft, so that he could transfer his precious racing birds from the cold, corrugated-iron structure in the back garden. The house, at 16 Distillery Lane, in chaotic condition, already consisted of Harry's ramshackle grocery shop on the ground floor and the flat of Handme Levy, a tailor, on the second.

The language is given over to event. The circumstantial detail, none of it irrelevant, creates both intimacy and a sense of relaxation between reader and author. The latter's personality is never foregrounded, not even in those stories told in the first person. 'Writing,' said Freud, 'is the record of an absent person.' Few writers manage to be intimate and yet absent to the degree that Brian Friel does. Alienation of the teller from the tale for the sake of the telling, this is his style. Such a style gives greater prominence to tone than to trope or figure. The most persistently identifiable tone in these stories is that of gossip and reminiscence, a peculiar blend of circumstantiality and nostalgia perfectly appropriate to a form in which there is an exact and welcome relationship already established between the teller and the listener, the author and the reader.

The prominence of the short story in modern Irish writing since Moore and Joyce has not been an entirely unmixed blessing. Yet at its best this form, more than any other, acknowledges and even exploits the existence of an audience. Although there are many radical differences between a folk-tale and a short story (most of them described by Walter Benjamin in his essay on Leskov) they at least share the conviction that the audience and the teller have a common cultural identity. In Ireland, this is intensified by the further appeal to a regional familiarity, recognisable in Joyce's evocation of Dublin, O'Connor's of Cork, and Friel's of Donegal-Derry. The tone subsequently produced has a great charm for the reader, since it allows him entry to the story on the ground of an assumed common knowledge and experience. Such a tone defines the distance between writer and reader by the pretence of abolishing it. Listen, for example, to the opening of *Ginger Hero:*

> At the time I'm thinking about, the year Billy Brogan and I bought our own fighting-cock and matched him against the best birds in Ireland, you would never have suspected that Annie and Min were sisters. Ten years earlier, when Billy married Annie and I married Min, they were as alike as two

11

peas, although, strangely enough, it was Min who was the softer of the two then.

The phrases 'At the time I'm thinking about,' 'you would never have suspected' and 'strangely enough' (with its nicely proleptic assumption) do not merely presume an audience. They also create one that is flatteringly granted the knowingness of the narrator who is observing his past self and history. The skill of the writing is such that we are eased into a world that is actually much stranger than it initially seems. Because of his manipulation of tone, because of the normative detail of his descriptions the author retards or defers our recognition of its oddity. Such a deferment is quite in keeping, for most of the stories in this selection are concerned with the ways in which people defer the vital existence for the neurotic or the joyless one. Life in these towns and villages is lived vicariously. The illusions of gold in the sea, of champion racing-pigeons or fighting cocks, of ultimate success or respectability do not simply disappear when their surrogate quality is acknowledged. Instead, they seem to exemplify the necessity of illusion in a society which so severely distorts the psychic life, most especially in its sexual aspect. We are not reduced by this to the banal observation that Irish social life is limited, hamstrung by convention and authority. Brian Friel's people live in a state of permanent and alert disappointment. What they are is never fulfilled by what they do. Yet the very discrepancy from which they suffer sharpens their sense of what they are. Because the society is defective their need for imaginative compensation is fostered and still it is not a blind but a conscious use of compensation. In these stories, Brian Friel explores that passage in modern Irish experience which has produced a great deal of our most memorable literature. It is the passage from a declining communal life to one in which the cult of the individual flourishes. The cult of the individual does not, paradoxically, lead to personal fulfilment. With its emphasis on internal freedom and its repudiation of the absorptive effects of a settled community, it most often makes a virtue of alienation and a fetish of integrity. This is the world of Moore and Joyce. Its preoccupations manifest themselves in a conscious experimentalism of technique and an almost ideological aggression towards the shabby Irish community. But another Ireland remained, its communal sense imperfect, but still intact. Synge explored it in drama, Mary Lavin, Sean O'Faolain, Frank O'Connor and Brian Friel explored it in the short story. In it, the failure to wholly be oneself is seen differently. It is not simply the place's fault or the individual's. It is a failure in the transaction between individual and society. It is one in which the awareness of individual distance from social intimacy has been born but in which it has not reached an extreme degree of dislocation. The strained connections of this tenderly understood relationship are probably best exemplified here in the title story.

The catastrophe which befell Nellie Doherty in her long struggle for respectability gives the community of the village of Drumeen an opportunity to behave with impeccable sympathy and also in accordance with the tacit assumptions of class and caste distinction. In such a society to become respectable is to attain selfhood. Vertically imposed upon the horizontals of class is the system of authority officially represented by the priest and unofficially by the diviner. It is a form of authority which does not derive from class although it operates within and has effects upon the class system. After science (the divers from the British naval base), and religion (Father Curran with his rosaries) and society (the organised efforts of the professional classes) have all failed, the diviner's magic takes over. Authority in its most basic form grows out of a sense of mystery but in its more quotidian form out of an awareness of status. The two aspects are epitomised in Nellie herself, who is devoted to status, and her drunken husband, whose mysterious past and unexplained drunkenness belong to the same world as the diviner—socially shabby yet indicative of forces beyond the merely social. The account of the dredging for the body, the swathes of light and darkness through which it is conducted, the sympathetic behaviour of the various groups which make up the community, is a fine example of Brian Friel's tact. The search for the body is an exploration of the community itself and of the individual's relation to it. It has the force of analysis but the tenor of description. It does not enunciate a moral, yet a morality is implied, one which colours the conduct of all concerned, bearing witness to the fact that the differences between individuals are not so pronounced as to deprive the community of a unified temperament. In this story, individuality is shown to be a social achievement; society is shown to be the home of individuality. Yet it is also a story in which the attempt to achieve selfhood fails and in which society's compensatory gesture of sympathy is not quite enough. In the end, only Nellie and the diviner are the outsiders. The crisis of the night has passed and the community's weakness is as manifest as her vulnerability. In this instance, Brian Friel has written a story which gains in significance as our historical retrospect upon it lengthens.

Since he is best known as a dramatist, it is only just that we should also give especial notice here to *Foundry House*, the story on which the play *Aristocrats* is obviously based. In the story, Joe Brennan refuses to surrender his ideal childhood vision of the Hogans—'A great family. A grand family'. Between the squalor of his own existence and the remembered splendour of theirs he has created a contrast which is both illusory and necessary. His imagination needs to believe in an alternative existence and thus the actual decrepitude of the Hogans cannot be admitted or articulated by him. It is a fine story, in which the only true aristocrat is the imagination. In the play, however, the illusions are broken and given up. Failure and collapse are publicly articulated after the catastrophic death of Justice O'Donnell. The disarray, emotional and financial, of his family allow no protection to myths or fantasies of the sort cherished by Casimir in *Aristocrats*. The imagery and the enactment on stage of speech stifled, speech electronically reproduced, speech rupturing silence (as in the case of Uncle George), demonstrate clearly how far Brian Friel the dramatist has moved beyond the world of Brian Friel the short-story writer. For in this and in other plays (*Living Quarters* and *The Freedom of the City* prominent among them) the relationship between community, familial and social, and the individual, alienated and stricken, has finally crumbled. Interaction between the two leads only to mutual destruction. In so far as a society depends upon the alliance between status and responsibility, it has become entirely defunct in the Ballybeg of Justice O'Donnell and in the Derry of British Law and Order. The friction between individual and group, between the demand for internal freedom and the system of embodied values is now intolerable. Here, in the development from stories to plays, Brian Friel's work registers a characteristic and irreversible development in modern Ireland.

The last sentence in *The Saucer of Larks* gives a pointer to the kind of morality with which these stories are suffused. The sergeant, somewhat embarrassed at having resisted the blank efficiency of the Germans who had come over to take away the remains of the German airman, turns away from the mock innocence of Guard Burke:

> For a man of his years and shape, he carried himself with considerable dignity.

'Dignity' is the word to fasten upon here. However relentless Brian Friel may be in his exposure of cowardice or illusion, he never forsakes the notion that human need, however artificially expressed, is rooted in the natural inclination towards dignity. To recognise the squalor and insufficiency of one's life by the creation of an alternative fiction is itself an expression of dignity, not simply a flight from reality. In these stories, moral qualities are the final reality. Circumstance may determine human choice in one respect, but choice governs the role of circumstance in another. The resource to go on living in the light of convictions that are too deeply instinctive to be fully articulated in speech and can only be partially articulated in action is denied to none of his people. They have to assume responsibility even as they lose hope, like Johnny in *Everything Neat and Tidy*, a story that would deserve inclusion on the strength of its final sentence alone:

> Chilled by this sudden personal disaster, he drove faster and faster, as if he could escape the moment when he would take up the lonely burden of recollections that the dead had fled from and the living had forgotten.

The nostalgic cadence of the sentence does not quite disguise the tonic effect of that moment when Johnny discovers he has to emerge from the world of behavioural role-playing into the world of adult conduct.

Although it is probably truer of Brian Friel's plays, it also illuminates something about the stories to say that they situate themselves upon a moment of crisis. The danger here is that the crisis may seem *voulu*, not quite congruent with the observed situation. However, what could be misunderstood as a taste for a melodramatic closure, seems to me something quite different. Even the quietest story here, *The Potato Gatherers*, shows the world to be a much harsher place than hope or fantasy could ever wish it. The brutal fact of money is more prominent here than in most of the others; but it is an undeniable pressure. More limiting than religion, more pressing than class distinction, work is something which the people in these stories attempt to convert into vocation or into a preliminary to the real life. This is, perhaps, the greatest seduction of all. The crisis in these stories and plays is brought about by the failure of work, the failure of long and unremitting effort to achieve a desired end. The crisis is not an exaggeration unless we allow to these stories what Adorno allowed to psycho-analysis when he said: 'In psycho-analysis nothing is true except the exaggerations.' Surely the decline of a traditional community, the assumption of a lonely individual burden, is mirrored most clearly in the disjunction between work and living? As Skinner in *The Freedom of the City* shows us, only the unemployed escape that dilemma, although they do so by exchanging it for another. The teachers and policemen, the shopkeepers and widows, the unemployed with their hobbies who populate these stories belong to a period of economic decline and exposure from which they inevitably receive psychological wounds. Perhaps their tragedy is that they feel these wounds as manifestations of their own personal incompetence; and perhaps on that account the illusions they breed are necessary to them.

So the enduring quality of these stories has nothing to do with an isolated moral quality, like dignity; nor has it to do with a general social decline and dilapidation. The quality resides in the tact and sympathy with which the interaction of these things is explored. It is a world of discriminations, not of decisions. When the narrator in *The Gold in the Sea* realises that Con, the creator of the fantasy, was asking him 'for something more important than money' we need not be at pains to decide what that something is. We see it as in a photographic negative, fully registered. It is the obverse of what hard, relentless work, old age and the need for money mean. It exists, as do they. To ratify its existence with such power is characteristic of Brian Friel's achievement. Con has given form to his desire and to that of the reader of his story. The actual has become real. This story and its companions enact that rare transmutation.

Seamus Deane

These stories appeared first
in
The New Yorker
and
The Saturday Evening Post.

The Diviner

During twenty-five years of married life, Nelly Devenny was ashamed to lift her head because of Tom's antics. He was seldom sober, never in a job for more than a few weeks at a time, and always fighting. When he fell off his bicycle one Saturday night and was killed by a passing motor-cycle, no one in the village of Drumeen was surprised that Nelly was not heartbroken. She took the death calmly and with quiet dignity and even shed a few tears when the coffin was lowered into the grave. After a suitable period of mourning, she went out to work as a charwoman, and the five better-class families she asked for employment were blessed for their prompt charity, because Nelly was the perfect servant—silent, industrious, punctual, spotlessly clean. Later, when others, hearing of her value, tried to engage her, they discovered that her schedule was full; all her time was divided among the bank manager, the solicitor, the dentist, the doctor and the prosperous McLaughlins of the Arcade.

Father Curran, the parish priest, was the only person she told she was getting married again, and he knew she told him only because she had to have a baptismal certificate and letters of freedom.

'He's not from around these parts, Nelly, is he?' the priest asked.

'He's not, Father.'

'Is he from County Donegal at all?'

'He's from the West, Father,' said Nelly, smoothing down the hem of her skirt. 'Of course, Mr. Doherty's retired now. He's not a young man, but he's very fresh-looking.'

'Retired?' the priest said promptingly.

'Yes, Father,' said Nelly. 'Mr. Doherty's retired.'

'And you'll live here in Drumeen with—with Mr. Doherty?'

'That is our intention, Father.'

'Well, I wish you every blessing, Nelly,' said Father Curran in dismissal, because he was an inquisitive man and Nelly was giving nothing away. 'I'll see you when you get back.' Then quickly—an old trick of his—'The wedding is in the West, did you say?'

'That has to be settled yet, Father,' said Nelly calmly. 'It will just be a quiet affair. At our time of day, Father, we would prefer no fuss and no talk.'

He took the hint and let her go.

Nelly Devenny became Nelly Doherty, and she and her husband moved into her cottage at the outskirts of the village. Drumeen's speculation on Mr. Doherty was wild and futile. What age was he? Was he younger than Nelly? What part of the West did he come from? What had he been—a train driver, a skipper of a fishing boat, a manager of a grocery shop, a plumber, a carpenter? Had he any relatives? Had he even a Christian name? Where had they met? Was it true that she had put an advertisement in the paper and that his was the only answer? But Nelly parried all their probings and carefully sheltered Mr. Doherty from their clever tongues. The grinding humiliation of having her private life made public every turnabout in bars and courthouses for twenty-five years had made her skilled in reticence and fanatically jealous of her dignity. He stayed in the house during the day while she worked, and in the evening, if the weather was good, they could be seen going out along the Mill Road for a walk, Nelly dressed entirely in black and Mr. Doherty in his gabardine raincoat, checked cap, and well-polished shoes, the essence of respectability. And in time the curiosity died and the only person to bring up the subject now and again was McElwee, the postman, who had been a drinking pal of Tom Devenny, her first husband. 'I'm damned if I can make head or tail of Doherty!' he would say to the others in McHugh's pub. 'A big, grown man with rough hands and dressed up in good clothes and taking walks like that—it's not natural!' And McElwee was also puzzled because, he said, Mr. Doherty had never received a letter, not even a postcard, since the day he arrived in Drumeen.

On the first Sunday in March, three months after their marriage, Mr. Doherty was drowned in the bog-black water of Lough Keeragh. Several of the mountainy Meenalaragan people who passed the lake on their way to last Mass in the village saw him fishing from Dr. Boyle's new punt, and on their way home from the chapel they found the boat, water-logged, swaying on its keel in the shallow water along the south shore. In it were Mr. Doherty's fishing bag, his checked cap, and one trout.

Father Curran went to Nelly's house and broke the news to her. When he told her, she hesitated, her face a deep red, and then said, 'As true as God, Father, he was out at first Mass with me,' as if he had accused her of having a husband who skipped Mass for a morning's fishing. (When he thought about her strange reaction later that day, he concluded that Mr. Doherty most likely had not been out at first Mass.) He took her in his car out to the lake and parked it at right angles to the shore, and there she sat in the front seat right through that afternoon and evening and night, never once moving, as she watched the search for her husband. When Father Curran had to go back to Drumeen for the seven o'clock devotions—in an empty chapel, as it turned out, because by then the whole of the village was at Lough Keeragh—he had not the heart to ask her to get out. So he borrowed the curate's car, and the curate took the parish priest's place beside Nelly. Every hour or so, they

21

said a rosary together, and between prayers Nelly
watched quietly and patiently and responded respectfully
to the curate's ponderous consolings.

Everyone toiled unsparingly, not only the people to
whose houses she went charring every day—her clients,
as she called them: Dr. Boyle; Mr. Mannion, of the
bank; Mr. Groome, the solicitor; Dr. Timmons, the
dentist; the McLaughlins—but the ordinary villagers,
people of her own sort, although many of them were
only names to her. Logan, the fish merchant, sent his
lorry to the far end of Donegal to bring back boats for
the job of dragging the lake; O'Hara, the taximan, sent
his two cars to Derry to fetch the frogmen from the
British Admiralty base there; and Joe Morris, the bus
conductor, drove to Killybegs for herring nets.

The women worked as generously as the men. They
condoled with Nelly first, each going to where she sat
in the parish priest's car and saying how deeply sorry
she was about the great and tragic loss. To each of them
Nelly gave her red, washer-woman's hand, said a few
suitable words of thanks, and even had the presence of
mind to inquire about a sick child or a son in America
or a cow that was due to calve. Then the women set up
a canteen in Dr. Boyle's boathouse and made tea and
snacks for the workers on the lake. Among themselves
they marvelled at Nelly's calm, at her dignified
resignation.

'The poor soul! As if one tragedy wasn't enough.'

'Just when she was beginning to enjoy life, too.'

'And they were so attached to each other, so complete
in themselves.'

'Have his people been notified?'

'Someone mentioned that to Nelly, but she said his
people are all dead or in England.'

'He must have got a heart attack, the poor man.'

'Maybe that . . .'

'Why? What did you hear?'

22

'Nothing, nothing. . . . Nobody knows for certain but himself and his Maker.'

'Is it true that he took the Doctor's boat without permission? That he broke the chain with a stone?'

'Sure, if he had gone to the Doctor straight and asked him, he would have got the boat and welcome.'

'Poor Nelly!'

'Poor Nelly indeed. But isn't it people like her that always get the sorest knocks?'

It was late afternoon before the search was properly organized. The mile-long lake was divided into three strips, which were separated by marker buoys. Each strip was dragged by a seine net stretched between two yawls. The work was slow and frustrating, the men unskilled in the job. Ropes were stretched too taut and snapped. The outboard motors got fouled in the weeds. Then dusk fell and imperceptibly thickened into darkness, and every available vehicle from Drumeen was lined up along the shore and its headlights beamed across the water. Submerged tar barrels were brought to the surface, the hulk of an old boat, the carcass of a sheep, a plough, and a cart wheel, but there was no trace of Mr. Doherty. At intervals of half an hour a man in shirt and trousers went to the parish priest's car to report progress to Nelly.

'Thank you,' she said each time. 'Thank you all. You are all so kind.'

And immediately the priest beside her would resume prayers, because he imagined that sooner or later she would break down.

Father Curran had just returned from devotions and released the curate when the two frogmen arrived. They were English, dispassionate, businesslike, and brought with them all the complicated apparatus of their trade. Their efficiency gave the searchers new hope. They began at the north end, one taking the east side, the other the west. Carrying big searchlights, they went down six times in all and then told Dr. Boyle and Mr.

Mannion that it was futile making any further attempts. The bottom of the lake, they explained, had once been a turf bog; the floor was even for perhaps ten yards and then dropped suddenly to an incalculable depth. If the body were lying on one of these shelves, they might have found it, but the chances were that it had dropped into one of the chasms, where it could never be found. In the circumstances, they saw no point in diving again. They warmed themselves at the canteen fire, loaded their gear in O'Hara's taxis, and departed.

The searchers gathered behind the parish priest's car and discussed the situation. Nelly's clients, the executives, who had directed operations up to this point, now listened to the suggestions of the workers. Some proposed calling the search off until daylight; some proposed pouring petrol on portions of the lake and igniting it to give them light; some proposed calling on all the fire brigades in the county and having the lake drained. And while the Drumeen people were conferring, the mountainy Meenalaragan men, who had raised the alarm in the first place and had stood, silent, watching, beside the drowned man's waterlogged boat throughout the whole day as if somehow it would divulge its secret, now bailed out the water and, armed with long poles, searched the whole southern end of the lake. When they had no success, they returned the boat and slipped off home in the darkness.

The diviner was McElwee's idea. The postman admitted that he knew little about him except that he lived somewhere in the north of County Mayo, that he was infallible with water, and that his supporters claimed that he could find anything provided he got the 'smell of the truth in it'.

'We're concerned with a man, not a spring,' said Dr. Boyle testily. 'A Mr. Doherty, who lies somewhere in that lake there. And the question is, should we carry on with the nets or should we wait until the morning and decide what to do then?'

'He'll come if we go for him,' McElwee persisted. 'They say he's like a priest—he can never refuse a call. But whether he takes the job on when he gets here—well, that depends on whether he gets the smell of the—'

'I suggest we drag the south end again,' said Groome, the solicitor. 'The boat was waterlogged when it was found; therefore, it can't have drifted far after the accident. If he's anywhere, that's where he'll be.'

'We'll wait until the morning,' said McLaughlin of the Arcade. 'There's no great urgency, is there? Wait until we have proper light.'

'I vote for getting the diviner,' said McElwee. 'He likes to work while the scent is hot.'

'It's worth trying,' said one of Logan's men. 'Anyhow, what are you going to do tomorrow—try the nets again? After what the frogmen told you?'

Most of the men agreed.

'All right! All right!' said Dr. Boyle. 'We'll get this fellow, whoever he is. But we'll tell Father Curran first.' They went round to the front of the car, and the Doctor spoke in to the priest.

'It has been suggested, Father,' he said, choosing his words as carefully as if he were giving evidence at an inquest, 'that we send for a diviner in County Mayo, a man who claims to be able to—to locate—'

'A what?' the priest demanded.

'A diviner, Father. A water diviner.'

'What about him?'

'It appears, Father, according to McElwee and some of the men here—it appears that this diviner has been successful on occasion in the past. We are thinking of sending for him.'

Father Curran turned to Nelly.

'They're going to send for a water diviner now,' he said, putting a little extra emphasis on the word 'now'.

'Whatever you say, Father,' said Nelly. 'I'll never be able to repay you for all your kindness this night.'

'Well, Father?' said the Doctor.

25

'It's up to yourselves,' said the priest. Then, in dismissal, 'Let us begin another rosary. "I believe in God the Father Almighty, creator of Heaven and earth . . ."'

McElwee and one of McLaughlin's apprentices set off after midnight for County Mayo. None of Nelly's clients offered a car, so they travelled in a fifteen-year-old van belonging to McElwee's brother-in-law. After they left, the searchers broke up into small groups, sat in the cars and lorries and tractors lined along the shore, turned off the headlights, and waited. The night was thick and breathless. The men talked of the accident and of Mr. Doherty. Each group knew something more about the man than had been known previously. In one car, it was known that his name was Arthur. Two lorries away, it was decided that Mr. Doherty was not as retiring as one might have thought; one night a boisterous bass voice was heard coming through Nelly's kitchen window. In the Arcade delivery van, someone said that Dr. Boyle was seen going into the cottage at least once a fortnight, and Nelly was never known to be sick. In one of the tractors, Nelly's frequent visits to the chemist were commented on. But these scraps of knowledge meant nothing; they were the kind of vague tales that might attach themselves to any stranger with a taste for privacy. The man at the bottom of the lake was still that respectable stranger in the good raincoat and the well-polished shoes.

The night was at its blackest when the pale lights of the returning van came bobbing over the patchy road. Immediately, fifty headlamps shot across the water and picked out tapering paths on the gleaming surface. Car doors slammed and the lake-side hummed with subdued excitement. Father Curran had been dozing. He opened his eyes and smacked his lips a dozen times. 'What? What is it?' he asked.

'They're back,' said Nelly, sitting forward in her seat. 'And they have him with them.'

26

The diviner was a tall man, inclined to flesh, and dressed in the same deep black as Nelly and the priest. He wore a black, greasy homburg, tilted the least fraction to the side, and carried a flat package, wrapped in newspaper, under his arm. The first impression was, What a fine man! But when he stepped directly in front of the headlights of one car there were signs of wear—faded, too active eyes, fingernails stained with nicotine, the trousers not a match for the jacket, the shoes cracking across the toecap, cheeks lined by the ready smile. He spoke with the attractive, lilting accent of the west coast.

McElwee and McLaughlin's apprentice, fluttering about the diviner like nervous acolytes, led him to Father Curran's car. He opened the door, removed his hat, and bowed to Nelly and the priest. His hair was carefully stretched across a bald patch. 'I am the diviner,' he said with coy simplicity.

Father Curran leaned across Nelly to get a closer look at him.

'What's your name? Who's your parish priest?'

He ignored the questions and addressed himself to Nelly, 'I will need something belonging to your husband, something that was close to his person—a tie, a handkerchief, a—'

'Will this do?' asked McElwee, thrusting the checked cap over the man's shoulder into the car.

'Yes, that will do,' the diviner said. 'Thank you.' Then, to Nelly, 'His name was Arthur Doherty.'

'Arthur Doherty,' Nelly repeated, almost in a whisper.

'And he was born and reared in the townland of Drung, thirteen miles north of Athenry.'

'Drung,' said Nelly. She licked her lips. 'Did you know him?'

'I travel the country and I meet many people. I will search for the stonemason, but I will promise nothing.'

'How did you know he was a stonemason? You must have known him.'

'In a manner of speaking. Just as I recognize you,' he said.

She leaned away from him. 'You don't know me! I never saw you before!'

'You are Nelly Devenny, a highly respectable and respected woman. You work for the best people in Drumeen.'

'That dirty toper McElwee,' McLaughlin of the Arcade broke in.

'I will do my best,' the diviner said, withdrawing from the car and smiling at her—a sly, knowing smile, a sort of wink without an eye being closed.

'Father!—' Nelly began. She clutched the priest's elbow, her face working with agitation.

Father Curran did not heed her; he was sniffing the air.

'Whiskey!' he announced. 'That man reeks of whiskey!'

'Father, what will he do? D'you think he's going to do anything, Father?'

'A fake! A quack! A charlatan! Get a grip on yourself, woman! We'll say another rosary and then I'll leave you home. They're wasting their time with that—that pretender!' And he blessed himself extravagantly.

Neither Dr. Boyle nor Mr. Groome nor Dr. Timmons nor Mr. Mannion nor McLaughlin of the Arcade volunteered to take the diviner out. McElwee and he went alone, the postman at the oars, the diviner sitting on the bench across the stern. The checked cap lay on his knees. He had removed the newspaper wrapping from his package, revealing a Y-shaped twig, and now he held it carelessly in his hands by the forked portion, the tail of the Y pointing away from him. The others gathered along the shore in the gloomy corridors between the headlights and watched them pull out. Before the boat was ten yards away from the edge of the water, Nelly left the priest's car for the first time that day and ran to join the watchers. The women gathered protectively around her.

The boat moved evenly up the lake. One minute it was part of the blackness, the next it was caught, exposed, frozen in a line of light projected by a headlight, then lost, then caught. Calmly, imperturbably, exasperatingly it went on revealing itself and losing itself, until the minutes of blackness seemed endless and the seconds of exposure mere flashes. But the pattern was regular—the vehicles were evenly spaced—and soon the eyes of the watchers knew to relax when the boat and blackness were one, but where it crossed a ribbon of light they devoured it, noted the new position of the oars, the slant of McElwee's back, the hunched, tensed shoulders of the diviner. No one spoke; no one dared speak. A word to a neighbour, a glance at one's watch, a look at Nelly's face and one might never find the punt again.

Then it disappeared. The watchers fastened on the next beam, waited, blinked, wondered had they missed it, stared again, murmured. Had it stopped? Where was it? Why the delay? Had it found something? Then it appeared again, moving slowly into the spotlight, first the bow, then McElwee, then the oars poised above the water, then the diviner, now standing rigid, his elbows bent, his hands at his chest, his head stiffly forward. There it sat, a yellow picture projected against the night. Seconds passed. A minute. Two minutes. Three minutes. To watch was pain. The picture dissolved, men and boat merging in a blur, then took shape again.

'Come out! Come out! Bring out the boat hooks!'

McElwee was on his feet, his face screaming into the light, his arms gesticulating wildly to an audience he could not see. 'He's here! Bring out the boats! He's here!'

No one stirred. Then, after a minute, a youth broke away from the crowd and leaped into a yawl, and another followed him, and then everyone was moving and calling for oars and lighting cigarettes and wading heedlessly out into the water. The women held Nelly's arms, because she was trembling violently.

The body lay in twenty feet of water directly below the diviner's quivering twig. They brought it in to the shore and carried it up the gravel immediately in front of Father Curran's car. There they laid it on top of a brown sail.

McElwee got down on his knees beside the body. He closed the eyes and the sagging mouth and knitted together the fingers of the rough hands. Then he adjusted the good gabardine raincoat and the trousers and placed the two feet together.

'He was a good man,' said the priest. He was standing beside the car door, close to the group of women that surrounded Nelly. He lifted his chin and allowed his eyelids to droop. 'He was a man who lived a quiet life and loved his God and his neighbours,' he said in his pulpit voice. 'At this moment, he is enjoying his just reward. At the hour of his demise, he was carrying his rosary beads—am I correct, McElwee?'

'I'll see, Father,' said McElwee.

He knelt again. While he worked, the men and women in the circle around the body looked away, gravely studying each other or staring off into the darkness beyond the cars. Then McElwee rose to his feet and moved quickly out of the circle, holding the dead man's belongings against his chest, his shoulders rounded as if to protect them. 'I—I—we'll have to look again, Father,' he said, facing away from the car. He took off his jacket and placed it on the ground and laid several objects on it. Then he folded the jacket around them.

'Did you find the beads?' the priest said.

'The clothes are soaking wet, Father. It's hard to get your hand into the pockets.'

'What do you have there?'

The postman straightened up and turned towards the light. 'There are these,' he said, holding something in his wet hands.

'Is that his wallet?'

'Yes. And the watch.'

'Give them to me.'

Someone handed the wallet and the watch to the priest, who gave them at once to Nelly.

'What else is there?' the priest asked.

'Nothing, Father.'

'There is something else in your jacket there, McElwee.'

'Show him, McElwee,' said the Doctor quietly.

McElwee looked at his jacket on the ground. Then he opened it. There were two dark-green pint whiskey bottles lying on it, side by side. One of them had no cork; and the other had been opened, but the cork was still in it.

'Ho-ho, so that's it!' said Father Curran. 'And what are you doing with two bottles?'

'I found them,' said McElwee quietly.

"He found them!' the priest cried. 'And what—' He saw the faces in the circle, and then realization hit him. He opened his mouth to speak again, but closed it without a word.

Imperceptibly, it was dawn, a new day vying with the priest's headlamps. No one spoke; no one moved. Then McElwee bent and folded his jacket over the bottles once more. He turned and glanced at the priest, and then, in a voice that was no more than a whisper but which carried clearly above the lapping of the water and the first uncertain callings of the birds, he said, 'We'll say a rosary for the repose of the soul of Arthur Doherty, stonemason, of Drung, in the County Galway'. He began the Creed, and they all joined him.

While they prayed, Nelly cried, helplessly, convulsively, her wailing rising above the drone of the prayers. Hers, they knew, were not only the tears for twenty-five years of humility and mortification but, more bitter still, tears for the past three months, when appearances had almost won, when a foothold on respectability had almost been established.

Beyond the circle around the drowned man, the diviner mopped the perspiration on his forehead and on the back of his neck with a soiled handkerchief. Then he sat on the fender of a car and waited for someone to remember to drive him back to County Mayo.

The Gold in the Sea

The *Regina Coeli* was the last boat to pull away from the harbour that evening. She was a twenty-footer of grace-less proportions, without sails, and with two sets of oars. I would have preferred to go in one of the bigger boats, with engines and a full-time crew, but the hotel barman told me they did not welcome passengers.

'Con's your man,' he said. 'What he catches won't glut the market. But he has travelled a bit, and himself and Philly and Lispy are a comical trio. Aye,' he added, smiling at some memory, 'even if you don't catch much, it's an education being out with Con.'

We were to have set out at eight, at the turn of the tide, but between one thing and another—each of the four of us stood a round of drinks, and then I called a fifth, because they had been so agreeable about taking me salmon fishing with them—it was almost nine before we climbed aboard. The July sun had withered and the Donegal hills were a sullen purple, but the whiskey drew us together, making us feel intimate and purposeful.

'By God, sirs, you'll get more fish tonight than you ever dreamed of!' said Con. 'Nothing like a choppy sea to make them jump.' He reclined in the stern, an elbow on the tiller, bald and garrulous as Odysseus. He was quick with energy, for all his seventy-two years. I sat in the bow, facing him. Between us were Philly and Lispy, each taut on an oar. They were young men in their thirties.

We had become acquainted in the bar of the hotel where I was spending my two weeks' holiday. There had been no diffidence between myself and the locals, because the appearance of the salmon in the bay two days previously created a happy urgency that made everyone in Ballybeg partners. After breakfast that morning, I had watched the boats return from their first night out, gunwales low in the water, the fishermen ponderous and slowmoving, as if they had risen, sated, from a huge meal. The tiny pier was crammed with vehicles—trucks, tractors, battered vans—and as soon as a catch was weighed and loaded on to a lorry the driver planted his elbow on the horn, stuck his head out of the window, and cleared a lane for himself with his oaths. The distraught official who supervised the noisy weighing had a moonface that was on the point of tears. 'Gentlemen, please!' he kept whimpering. Young boys on their way to school peered down into the half-deckers and saw five-, ten-, and twenty-pound salmon that would be ten-, twenty-, and forty-pound salmon when their friends from the far side of the mountain heard about them. The vehicles scraped one another. Tyres skidded on the wet, cobbled pier. Only the conquering fishermen were calm and aloof. In twos and threes, they came up the steep road to the village with the walk of kings.

Philly was Con's nephew. They lived in different cottages on a jointly owned five-acre farm. Con was a bachelor ('But if I had a penny for every woman I handled, by God, sirs, I'd be a millionaire!'), and his nephew, he told the bar with unnecessary gusto, was the father of seven daughters. 'But he'll sire a son yet, never worry!' Lispy, I learned, lived with two maiden aunts who doted on him, but not to the extent of allowing him to bring a bride into the house. He was a shy man, whose quietness suggested depth and whose speech gave no explanation for his nickname. Perhaps he inherited it. When Lispy had gone to the toilet, Con told me that

34

Lispy got mad drunk once a year, on Saint Patrick's Day, when he chased the two screaming aunts out of the house and over the stunted fields. 'Just to assert his rights,' Con concluded. 'A saint when sober, but inclined to be sporty on that one occasion.' All three men were full-time farmers and part-time fishermen, and by any standards they were very poor.

Two miles out from the harbour, free from the shelter of the headland, we were struck by a brisk Atlantic wind. We were now part of an impenetrable blackness.

'At this very moment, friend,' Con proclaimed, 'you're sitting on top of more gold than there is in the vaults of Fort Knox.'

'We'll get our share,' I said, thinking he was referring to the salmon, which he had described earlier as being so plentiful that you could dance a reel on their backs and not wet a toe.

'Real gold!' he said. 'At this very spot, on an August morning in 1917, the *Bonipart* was sunk by a German submarine on her way from England to the U.S.A. Fifty fathoms straight below us. A cargo of bullion.'

'*Boniface*,' corrected Philly.

'There's no smoke without fire,' said Lispy. He had a weakness, I discovered, for proverbs that apparently had relevance only to private thoughts of his own.

'She was slipping down along the coast,' Con went on, 'when the Huns caught up with her here. By God, sirs, you've got to hand it to them Germans!'

'Was it never recovered?' I asked.

'*Boniface*,' repeated Philly doggedly. 'He always gets the name wrong.'

'Two shells done it,' said Con. 'One in the bows that made her rise up like a stallion, and then one midships. She went down like a knife.'

'And you don't know for sure what she was carrying. No one knows that,' said Philly.

'Just two shells,' said Con. 'And—bang!—requiescat the *Bonipart*.'

'*Boniface,*' said Philly, but without heart.

'Enough gold to develop all the underdeveloped countries of the world—including Alaska.'

'The last straw broke the camel's back,' said Lispy mildly.

'Right below our feet. By God, sirs, it's a wonderful thought, too, isn't it? It's there and it's safe and no one has laid a finger on it. Happy as an old lark.'

While the whiskey was still active in me, I made a few confident calculations. Assuming we caught a hundred fish (this was modest; that morning the *St. Brendan* had waddled into port with three hundred), averaging ten pounds per fish, our night's work, at the current wholesale price of eight shillings and sixpence per pound, would earn us four hundred and twenty-five pounds. I did the calculation again, because this seemed a lot of money, but I got the same result. Then, as one does when easy wealth presents itself, I built myself a chalet above Ballybeg, bought a boat, hired a crew, set up a canning factory and an export business, and was getting down to the details of an advertising campaign when the ghostly hulk of a long powerboat suddenly rose out of the water beside me, towered over me for a second, and vanished, thrumming in the blackness. I was instantly cold and sober.

'By the look of them, that was the McGurk brothers,' said Con casually. 'Damned near rammed us, didn't they?'

'Why haven't they a light?' I almost shouted.

'A light!' said Philly, with contempt. 'And have the patrol boat down on them for fishing without a licence? Are you mad?'

'Why don't they take out a licence?' I demanded.

'Costs money,' said Philly flatly.

'A stitch in time saves nine,' said Lispy.

'You mean to say,' I went on, 'that for all we know there may be dozens of boats all around us, not one with a light? And all of them poaching?'

36

'Not dozens,' said Philly. 'Maybe three or four.'

'And what happens if they get caught—if they don't drown us and themselves first.'

'Boat's confiscated. Gear's confiscated. Up to six months in jail.'

'Too good for them!' I shouted. 'It's a disgrace having—'

'By my reckoning, sirs,' Con broke in, 'we're near the Stags, and it's about time we shot the net. You can argue to your heart's content when we're drifting. Ship the oars, sirs, and let's get the net out.'

I heard him fasten the tiller with a rope and the handles of the oars speared towards me. I reached out to catch them, and then it dawned on me for the first time that we had no light either.

I had examined the net earlier in the day. It was three miles long, four feet deep, made of nylon, and manufactured in Japan. It was designed to float about twelve inches below the surface. Con had explained that these Japanese nets were new to the Irish market, and that they were so transparent the fish couldn't see them even in the daytime. I asked him if this meant that salmon fishing could now be done in the daytime, at which he laughed scornfully and replied that sure God and the world knew that you fished salmon only at night. I left it at that.

Now, while the boat drifted, the net was fed out from the stern. The job took the best part of an hour. The blackness was so dense that the three fishermen had identity only by their voices. Con, I gauged, was on the middle bench, issuing instructions, and Philly and Lispy were throwing out the net. They talked incessantly.

'Hurry up, sirs! It'll be dawn before you know.'

'Shut up!'

'The best salmon in the world are got in Peru.'

'How would you know?'

'I seen men in my day grilling a seventeen-pounder over an open fire near the town of Pisco, if you ever heard of it.'

'It's an ill wind that blows nobody good.'

'Come on, sirs! The seven daughters and the two aunts will think you've emigrated.'

'For a man with such a big mouth, how is it you never got a thump across it during your famous travels?'

'We'll fill the boat tonight, sirs. I'll settle for nothing short of a boatload.'

'Look before you leap.'

'Gold, sirs. Cast out the net and bring in the gold.'

'Fit you better to talk less and work more.'

'This will be a lovely catch. And I've seen apples in Oregon that were as big as a bishop's head. And I seen oranges in San Paulo that two men, eating steady, couldn't get through in a week.'

'You and your stories. There's nothing as hateful as an old man that never stops talking.'

'Faraway hills look green.'

'This is the work'll put muscles on your backs, sirs. A season of this, Philly boy, and you'll father half-a-dozen sons.'

'A blathering old woman! Hateful!'

'There's no smoke without fire. Oh, God, no—no smoke at all.'

When the net was all out, its end was secured to the stern. Then the three men moved back to their first positions, and the long, long wait began. For the next hour, no one spoke, not even Con. Despite the sound of wind and sea and the rheumaticky groans of the *Regina Coeli,* we seemed to be encased in silence. The elements made their blustering noises above and beyond, but in and around our floating arena there was a curious stillness. In the drifting blackness of the night I could hear Philly's deep, regular breathing and the coins rattle in Con's trousers every time he searched for matches to light his pipe. It was a strange sensation, floating in blackness across an unknown sea, with men one couldn't see but whose intimate movements one could hear distinctly. And as time crept by, my senses sharpened and became responsive to a shift in the direction of the boat, to the slightest movement of a body, almost to the very presence of the fish beneath us. It was a strange, thrilling perceptivity, like playing blindman's buff for the first time as a child. I wondered if the others experienced it, and as soon as this thought occurred to me I found myself going absolutely still, opening my mouth so that even my breathing would not be audible, speculating with absurd cunning that my thinking might be somehow perceptible.

Con's booming voice smashed the secrecy, and the noise of the wind and the seas crashed in.

'It was in the winter of 1918,' he said, 'and I was assing about in the region of a town called Fort Good Hope on the Mackenzie River, if you ever heard of it.'

'I did not,' said Philly curtly.

'And there was no work, and the whole damned place was under sixteen foot of snow, and there was a famine in my belly and not a cent in my pocket.'

'Oh-ho, oh-ho,' said Lispy mildly.

'So bloody bad was that winter, sirs, that the wolves came down from the hills, down into the very streets of Fort Good Hope, and ate all before them.'

'Pity they missed you—if you were there at all.'

'Anyhow, to cut a long story short, the townsfolk held a meeting, and it was agreed that they would pay a dollar out of the public funds for every wolf's head that was brought in to McFeterson's trading station. And a dollar in them days was something, sirs. You wouldn't light your pipe with a dollar in them days.' He waited for a comment. None came.

'So off I went into the hills with a Winchester—'

'Through sixteen foot of snow!' said Philly.

'—shot two dozen wolves, cut the heads off them, and carried them back to Good Hope.'

'Will you listen to the man!'

'Still waters run deep.'

'Presented my load to old Robbie McFeterson and said, "Twenty-four dollars, Robbie, please." Robbie counted the heads and gave me my money. And then says he, "Here, sonny boy, take them heads out the back and bury them." And that's what I done. Buried them in the snow behind the trading station, and then went back in and bought food and whiskey and had a hell of a week to myself. But when the week was up, I was broke again and hungry again, and my tongue was out a mile for a drink. So what did I do, friend?'

'You loaded the Winchester, Con,' I said.

'I went down that Sunday night to the plot behind the trading station and dug up them heads and the next morning presented them to Robbie! That's what I done! And he paid me—twenty-four dollars! And I done the same thing the following Monday and the following Monday and the following—'

'Damned things would have been rotten after four days!' Philly said.

'In twenty foot of snow, man? Fresh as a daisy! And old Robbie never suspected a thing. As straight a man as ever drew breath.'

'A man who never told a lie,' Philly said bitterly.

'By God, sirs, you've got to hand it to them Canadians!'

About two in the morning, we had cold tea and huge hunks of homemade bread. The tea tasted of disinfectant, and I furtively emptied mine over the side. I chewed mouthfuls of the bread until it became a thick, dry paste in my mouth, and then I tried to swallow it in a piece, without tasting it, the way one swallows medicine. When I had got through my ration, Lispy insisted I share his—'The old aunts aren't too bad at the soda bread'—and I took two more slices. One I ate with effort. The other I dropped into the sea, and then wondered if it might not get caught in the net and be hauled back into the boat later.

After we had eaten, Con resumed his tales of his travels; Philly must have dozed, because his uncle held forth without interruption. Lispy threw in an occasional proverb, perhaps to show that he was awake and listening. I was cold and tired and eager for the night to end. My dreams of a salmon industry had lost some of their sparkle.

It was still pitch black when they began to haul the net. It was then about 4 a.m., and the darkness was as dense as ever, but one felt it had lost its terrible permanence; a change was imminent. The blackness would soon be fragmented. When they began to haul the net —Philly and Lispy again doing the donkey work, Con instructing and encouraging, and me mumbling an occasional commendation just to establish my participation—we rediscovered the purpose and intimacy that had animated us when we had set out. We knew again that out of the black, invisible waters we were about to draw in a small fortune in fish. It was a lovely feeling.

'She's a grand boat, this,' Lispy said to me with sudden friendliness. 'And her name is *Regina Coeli*. That's Latin, and it means "Star of the Sea".'

They were still hauling when the sky and sea became distinct. The sky was a fuzz of mist that ringed our craft at a discreet distance. The last fifty yards of net had still to be pulled in when the sky suddenly broke into black and orange and grey streaks. I could see Con's bald head glistening with salt water, and Philly's and Lispy's yellow waterproofs billowing like sails in the morning breeze. Now all the net was lifted. The young men straightened up and waited to get their breath back, and Con released the fish from the mesh. His broad shoulders concealed his movements. I could not see how many we had landed.

'Well?' said Philly.

'Salmon caught in the net, friend, is never as good to eat as salmon caught with a fishing line,' said Con. 'And I'll tell you why. When they get caught in the net, they

41

can't breathe, and their lungs burst, and unless you get them and pack them right off, they go bad very quick.'

'How many's in it?' said Philly impatiently.

'But if you catch a fish with a rod and line,' Con went on, 'you kill him before his lungs burst, and he's a better fish to eat—far better.'

'I asked you—how many are there?'

Con straightened and grimaced up at the sky. 'Six,' he said flatly. 'There's six in it. Six wee ones.'

'Oh-ho, oh-ho,' said Lispy.

Philly spat out a curse. There was a long silence.

'Right, sirs!' Con announced suddenly in a new, vigorous voice. 'Back to the oars, and home to the daughters and the aunts. There'll be another day. Oh, by God, there'll be another day!'

He moved back to the stern, and Philly and Lispy each took an oar, and we headed for home, taking our direction from a cold, grey sky. Six small fish, I calculated, would fetch about fifteen pounds—five pounds for each of the three men. Then, I remembered Con telling me that the Japanese net cost eighty pounds, more than half of which had still to be paid. He said it could be lost in a storm or destroyed by seals before it had been paid off. To balance my rising sympathy, I told myself that they were not, after all, real fishermen, but poachers; that they had no right to fish and so could not be disappointed with their catch. But it was no time for assessments. The sky had grown brilliant and the headland was strong and permanent ahead of us. The night was a failure. I was wet and hungry and miserable.

'At this very moment, friend,' Con proclaimed suddenly, 'you're sitting on top of more gold than there is in the vaults of Fort Knox.'

'You were telling me about that,' I said coldly.

'A cargo of bullion. Heading for the States.'

'Tell him about the salvage ship,' said Philly.

'None of us knows what it got—if it got anything,' replied Con sharply.

'Tell him all the same.'

'The proof of the pudding is in the eating,' said Lispy.

'What's this about a salvage ship?' I asked.

'Five years ago,' said Con, addressing me but watching Philly and Lispy with his sailor's eyes, 'on a clear spring morning, a Dutch salvage vessel dropped anchor at this very spot and didn't move away for twenty-seven days. She had divers and equipment and all the rest of it. But none of us knows did she get anything.'

'They weren't here for the good of their health,' said Philly. He turned to me. 'What do you think?'

'Take my word for it,' Con broke in. 'They got nothing. Didn't I watch them through the glasses day and night? And didn't I tell you dozens of times they pulled up nothing but seaweed?'

'You couldn't swear to it.'

'For God's sake, I'm not a swearing man. I'm telling you—the gold's still down there in the *Bonipart.*'

'*Boniface.*'

'Call it what you like. It's all there, happy as an old lark.'

'Maybe you're right,' said Philly, with surprising amiability. 'I'm not saying you're wrong. All I'm saying is that we don't know for sure.'

'Take my word for it,' said Con with finality. 'We're sitting on a gold mine.' He spoke with such authority that somehow we all felt that he must be right.

We were the first to tie up at the harbour. The place was deserted, silent in the clean morning light. There was only the sharp smell of old fish and the light, echoey sound of the water under the dock. Now that we were on land again, our bodies were slow and unsure with fatigue. I thanked them for taking me with them, and we shook hands formally. Con held me by the elbow until the young men were out of earshot.

'It wasn't much good, was it?' he asked.

'I enjoyed it, Con,' I said.

43

In the daylight, he looked every one of his seventy-two years— an old man with tired eyes. 'The point is,' he said, 'the fish are there, a bloody harvest of them. You saw for yourself the catches them big boats landed. What we need is an outboard. That's what we need. I keep telling the boys that. "The fish is there," I say to them when they lose heart.'

He stood looking back at the sea, still holding my arm. Then he spoke in a rush. 'I told you a lie about the *Bonipart*.'

'Yes?' I said cautiously. I thought he was going to ask me for money.

'The Dutchmen cleaned her out from head to foot. I seen it all through the glasses from the point of the headland. They took cartloads of stuff off her. Didn't leave a bolt on her.'

'And was she really carrying bullion?'

He didn't hear me, but went on as if I hadn't spoken.

'I don't want Philly or Lispy to know this. It's better for them to think it's still there. They're young men. . . . You see, friend, they never got much out of life. Not like me.'

His voice trailed off, and I suddenly understood that he was asking me for something more important than money.

'You saw the world, Con,' I said. 'You've been everywhere.'

'Damned right I have!' he said. 'Canada, the United States, South America—right round the world before I was twenty!'

He turned, and we walked off the dock and started up the hill together.

'By God, sirs,' he said, 'You've got to hand it to them Dutchmen!'

The Widowhood System

The very day his mother was buried, Harry Quinn set about converting the two attic rooms, from which she had ruled the house for the last nineteen years of her impossible dotage, into a model pigeon loft, so that he could transfer his precious racing birds from the cold, corrugated-iron structure in the back garden. The house, at 16 Distillery Lane, in chaotic condition, already consisted of Harry's ramshackle grocery shop on the ground floor and the flat of Handme Levy, a tailor, on the second. Handme—short for Hand Me Down the Moon (he was six and a half feet tall if he was an inch)—helped with the tasks of reconstruction, because midwinter was an even slacker time than usual in the tailoring business and because he was already in arrears to Harry, his landlord. Fusilier Lynch gave a hand, too, out of the goodness of his heart. For six days, the three men worked, stopping only to eat the meals that Judith Costigan, who lived next door in No. 15, made for them. When the job was complete, they carried the thirty-six pigeons in, two at a time, each man making six journeys out to the garden, in through the shop, past the smirking tailor's dummies in Handme's living room, and up to the top of the house. Then they drank in celebration. They drank, as they did after every race, win or lose, in the kitchen behind the shop.

'It's a powerful loft,' said Handme. 'Height and space and light.'

'A castle,' murmured the Fusilier.

'You waited one hell of a long time to get them inside, Harry,' said Handme. 'But it was worth waiting for.'

'A palace,' said the Fusilier.

Harry suffered from running eyes. They were never dry. Strangers who went into his shop were disturbed by the sight of the weeping shopkeeper. 'Now I'm going to tell you something, boys,' he announced, mopping his tears with a soiled handkerchief. 'Something that's been in my nose for nineteen years.'

'You're going to marry Judith!' said Handme.

'I'm going to produce the best racing pigeon Mullaghduff has ever seen. As a matter of fact, boys, I'm going to breed the first local pigeon ever to win the All Ireland Open Championship.'

Handme's face was permanently fixed in the expression a man has immediately before he sneezes—mouth open, teeth bared, eyes wide, forehead wrinkled. On him, it became a look of wild delight and anticipation. That, on top of a thin, gangling body, made the young girls of the town scared stiff of him. 'By God, Harry, you will, too!' he cried, 'Won't he, Fusilier?'

The Fusilier was short, stocky, silent. He was in his late forties, the youngest of the three bachelors. He was better at greyhounds and whippets than at birds, but a good all-rounder. 'How?' he asked cautiously.

'By science,' said Harry. 'I'll get my bird, train it the way you would train an athlete, feed it right, exercise it right, get to understand its psychology. It's a matter of science.'

'By God, you're right, Harry!' said Handme. 'The All Ireland Open, no less! Eh?'

'And where do you propose getting this wonder bird in the first place?' asked the Fusilier.

Harry paused before he answered. 'I'm going to breed it,' he said.

'Huh!' The Fusilier laughed drily and began examining his corduroy riding breeches, which were bald at the knees.

'I'm going to breed it scientifically,' Harry went on calmly, 'according to the theories, principles, and practice of Gregor Johann Mendel.'

'Is that the Galway buck that raced the wee grey hen last—?' Handme began.

'Gregor Johann Mendel says—and in case you boys never heard of him he is a priest and a scientist—he says that a racing pigeon isn't a racing pigeon at all. A racing pigeon, he says, is a bundle of bloody genes. Get the right genes, says he, and you have the winner of the All Ireland cooing in your lap.'

'What club is he in, this Mendel fella? Where's his loft?' the Fusilier asked.

'What I've been doing all my life, what every fancier in this country has been doing all their lives,' Harry went on softly, 'is mating the best cocks with the best hens. Quality with quality, stamina with stamina, speed with speed. And we've all been wasting our time.' He leaned across the kitchen table and wiped his eyes so as to get a moment's clear vision of his friends' faces. 'According to the Mendelian theory, when you breed champ with champ the offspring generally tends towards the average of the species, unless both members to the union are ...' He faltered. The quotation he had learned from the Pigeon Fanciers Post began to fade. The word 'homozygous' pirouetted before his mind and vanished.

'Anyhow,' he went on, 'the point is this: Quality with quality is no guarantee of quality young ones. Haven't we proved that ourselves? So what I'm going to do now, boys, is the very opposite: fast cock to slow hen, lazy cock to active hen. Until sooner or later I'll have a national winner in my loft. Trial and error—the scientific method. And, by God, boys, with the old woman out of the road and the place to myself, there's nothing to stop me now!'

Later that night, when Harry invited his friends into Judith's house for supper, Handme told her of Harry's scheme. She laughed and said, 'Good for you Harry!'

47

and went on making them a huge feed of rashers and eggs. There never was a more eventempered, more placid woman than Judith Costigan. When her young scut of a brother, Billy, whom she had reared, sailed for Canada one August morning, leaving her with no means of support except the knitting she did for the glove factory, she laughed and said, 'Aren't I lucky to have a roof over my head?' When old Mrs Quinn became bedridden and summoned Judith to feed and clean her, Judith laughed and said, 'It's the least I could do for a neighbour'. And on those Saturday nights after a race had been lost or won, when Harry, Handme, and the Fusilier had drunk themselves silly and adjourned to Judith's to round the night off, she laughed most heartily because Harry invariably said to her, 'Judith Costigan, someday I'm going to ask you to marry me—someday when I'm good and sober.' It was a funny sight to see Harry swaying in the middle of the kitchen floor, his hand on his chest, his cheeks streaming with tears, and Judith, plump, smooth, hazel-eyed, fresher-looking than her forty-four years, nodding her head and laughing generously at him. It was so funny that Handme Levy would forget himself and begin to do a jig, until his spinning head could no longer control his long, miserable shanks and he would fall into a chair and grimace wildly at the ceiling. Then the Fusilier would get maudlin about his time in the British Army—when, as he said, 'for four long years my stomach was starved for the whiff of a greyhound'. When they had sobered, they would crawl home, and they would not call on Judith again until the next race day, or until they wanted a well-cooked meal.

His mother was not dead a year when the laziest of Harry's hens, which he had paired with a cock with a broken wing, laid two white eggs. The awkward father knocked one of the eggs out of the nest, and it smashed on the concrete floor. Out of the other egg came the bird that Harry was waiting for. Of course he did not know this until he saw it on the wing. But he knew then. Then there was no doubt at all. It was a small pigeon, blue-grey, with a white neck and a flat-topped head. Its great pectoral muscle filled its breast and stirred gently against the hand. Its back was broad and strong and straight. Its legs were short. Its full, ovoid body was smothered in velvety feathers.

Handme examined it one Sunday morning. Then he passed it to the Fusilier. Harry waited for their comments. The lofts were open, and the birds, in squadrons of fifteen, flew at the same height as the chapel bells, rolling over the tops of the pines and across the river and out over the barley fields and back to the peaks of the pines again.

'It's a good bird, all right,' said Handme. 'How does it take off?'

'Clean and straight,' said Harry.

'Any trouble in trapping it?'

'None. It lands on the platform and drops right down.'

'Aye, it's a good bird, all right,' said Handme. 'Isn't it, Fusilier?'

The Fusilier handed the bird back to Harry. 'It's a cock,' he said.

'It's what?' Handme squealed his surprise.

'I know it's a cock,' said Harry with dignity.

'But—but—Harry, you're not thinking of racing a cock, are you?' Handme spluttered. 'I mean to say, you never raced a cock in your life—it was always hens. The natural system . . . back to the nest . . .'

'And did I ever do anything worthwhile racing the natural system?' snapped Harry, suddenly angry. 'Isn't that what all the fanciers round here are doing—racing the natural system? A flock of bloody turkeys waddling back to a cosy seat on eggs. And did any man of them ever win a national trophy in his natural life? Well, did they or did they not?'

'Not that I know of,' said Handme, subdued more by Harry's voice than by his argument.

'So,' said Harry quietly. 'I'm going to try the widow-hood system. And I'm going to make a job of it.'

'You will, too,' said Handme. 'It's a grand bird, all right.'

'Have you mated him yet?' asked the Fusilier.

'Not yet,' said Harry. 'I'm going to mate him with a wee fat red hen. I saw him eyeing her.'

'Is he keen?' said the Fusilier.

'How the hell would I know? He didn't confide in me!'

'There's nothing wrong with the widowhood system,' said the Fusilier calmly, looking out across the still, Sabbatical town, 'only for the drawbacks. I seen cocks in my day that were so eager to get back to the hen they battered themselves against the basket and wore themselves out, so that they were too tired to race. And I seen cocks in my day that didn't give a damn if they never saw the hen again. If you want a sure performance, give me a hen every time. A hen will always hurry back to the nest. It's not called the natural system for nothing.'

'And what the hell do you think the widowhood system is?' said Harry, wiping his cheeks with the cuff of his jacket. 'What could be more natural than for a cock to fly back to its mate?'

'True for you, Harry,' Handme agreed, although he was thinking of the young girls of the town scattering in all directions when he met them coming out of the glove factory.

'Anyhow,' Harry went on, 'I'm sending him to Omagh next Friday week for a tryout the next day. You'll see then if I'm right.'

'Thirty miles is too far,' said the Fusilier. 'Send him to Omagh and that's the last you'll see of him.'

'Maybe the Fusilier's right,' said Handme. 'Why not try Strabane for a first outing? Fifteen miles is plenty for a first outing.'

'And you can't race him till he's mated first,' said the Fusilier.

'And you're not sure that the red hen'll have him,' said Handme.

Harry blinked his eyes and glared from one to the other. 'You two,' he said, his voice breaking with frustration, 'think you know everything! But you know damn all! This is my bird! And I'm going to race him from Omagh! And he'll mate for me! And he'll race for me—scientifically, by the widowhood system!'

He flung open the trapdoor and held the bird on the palms of his hands beneath it, as if it were an offering. It spread its wings, hesitated a second, then rose up and out into the spring air, where it joined a squadron of fifteen and tumbled in the waves of the singing bells.

Handme and the Fusilier were right; Omagh was too far. But in everything else they were wrong. On the Tuesday before the race, Harry had paired the bird with the red hen, and she had acquiesced. And on the day before the race, he had held the cock close to the hen until the cock's muscles tensed, but he had not allowed them to breed. Then he slipped the rubber race ring round the pigeon's leg, thrust the bird into the basket, and carried it down to the railway station. The know-all Fusilier was wrong in that detail, too; the bird did not batter itself against the sides of the cage. Indeed, Harry would have been happier if it had shown even some anxiety at being separated from its mate. But it was not an excitable bird, he consoled himself, and surely that was a good thing.

Four other pigeons from the local club were entered for that race, and the best of them, Joe McSorley's checkered hen, clocked in seconds after 11.00 a.m. Major O'Donnell's two birds arrived next, at 11.15 a.m. and at 11.18 a.m. At 11.23 a.m., Harry saw Patsy Boyle's ten-year-old hen flit over the pine trees, as fresh as if she were starting out, and she had eight miles farther north to travel. This meant that her velocity was almost as good as the velocity of the Major's birds. Even though all the birds were released from the same place at the

51

same time, each had a different distance to travel back to its own loft, and its speed over its own distance was what mattered. As soon as the birds were liberated, each owner set his timing clock in motion, and as soon as his bird returned he dropped its leg ring into the mechanism and thus stopped the clock. After the race, these clocks were all submitted to the club for examination, and the different times and distances were calculated and the winner determined.

The Angelus bell rang at noon. Harry went up to the loft for the eighth time. His cock had not returned. He boiled potatoes for his lunch and ate them. He washed the counter in the shop, mopped the floor, and disposed of fly-papers that had been hanging from the ceiling since last summer. He climbed the stairs again. Still no bird. Then he threw a handful of maize inside the trap-door, went down to Handme's bedroom, and shook him awake. 'Keep an eye on the shop!' he shouted into the startled eyes. 'I'm away out for a pint.'

'The bird—is he back?'

'He'll come back in his own good time,' said Harry over his shoulder.

His own good time was at six-thirty that evening, and by then Harry and Handme and the Fusilier were sozzled. It was the Fusilier who found him perched in the loft. The two others heard the Fusilier stumbling down the stairs, singing to the bird, ' "You are my sunshine, my only sunshine. You make me happy when skies are grey." '

'Welcome back, wee cock!' cried Handme. 'Had you a nice holiday in New York?'

'Don't let me see him!' Harry called, crying into his hands. 'He disgusts me—that's what he does, disgusts me.'

'Sh-h-h,' said the Fusilier. 'He's back, isn't he? Isn't that all that matters? Where's the clock? Gimme the timing clock and we'll drop his ring in—just for the record.' He kissed the bird gently on the back.

'Take him away!' Harry called. 'He disgusts me.'

'Hens every time,' said Handme. 'For reliability and dependability and—'

'Fling him in the loft out of my sight! I still have some bloody pride.'

'Now, now, now, boys,' said the Fusilier, holding the bird to his cheek.

'He went and had a holiday on top of the Statue of Liberty!' said Handme. 'That's what he done!'

'But he'll race!' said Harry. 'By God, he'll race before I'm done with him, or I'll know why!'

'He's nothing but a bundle of beans,' said Handme, believing he was quoting Gregor Johann Mendel.

'Yessir, he'll race! I'm not beaten yet, not by a long chalk!'

' "You are my sunshine, my only sunshine," ' sang the Fusilier as he made his way up the stairs again.

That night ended in Judith's house. After she had fed them, she saw Handme's dance and heard the Fusilier's reminiscences about Army life and listened to Harry's tearful proposal. They did not leave her until almost three in the morning, and she was still laughing when she said good night to them.

In the following two months, the bird was raced three times—from Monaghan; from Campbelltown, in Scotland; and from Wexford. Each time, Harry set his timing clock but never submitted it to the local club for scrutiny after the bird had returned. When the other fanciers would ask him was he competing or was he not, he would reply that he was entering but not competing. 'I just want him to get some practice,' he would say, 'but I don't want him to stretch himself until the All Ireland.' And they would answer, 'Suit yourself, Harry. It's your bird,' and wink slyly at one another.

Handme came up with several explanations for the cock's indifferent performances. 'I've been studying its skull, Harry,' he said, the day after the Monaghan outing. 'That's where your trouble lies.'

53

'Aye?'

'It's my opinion, Harry, that the head isn't developed right, with the result that the brain is being squeezed in its cavity.'

'Is that your opinion?'

'Doesn't it sound sensible? I think that if we could get some way to develop its skull, there wouldn't be that pressure on its brain. And if its brain wasn't being squeezed, it could concentrate better on flying.'

'D'you know what I think, Handme?' Harry replied, with commendable control. 'I think that if you stuck to your sewing it might suit all of us a lot better.'

After the Campbelltown trial, Handme's explanation was that the pigeon was allergic to salt water. 'It's my belief that he was going like a bomb until he was over the North Channel. Then the salt water went for his sinuses and his respiration breathing was done for.'

And when the bird took over sixteen hours to return from Wexford on a day that was calm and clear and sunny, Handme said, 'Harry, I've got the answer now. He's tired of the wee hen! Give him another hen and you'll find he'll be back before he leaves!'

'He wouldn't be interested in another hen,' said Harry.

'He wouldn't what?' said Handme, baring his teeth. 'Pigeons are no different to the rest of us!'

'For your information,' said Harry, remembering a quotation from the Post, 'pigeons tend to be monogamous.'

'Is that what Father Mendel says?'

'It is,' said Harry wearily.

'You may be sure! That's what's wrong with us in this country—bloody-well priest-ridden! And if you ask me, he should know nothing about all that. So take my advice, Harry, and get him another mate.'

'It's in him,' said Harry, not answering the tailor. 'It's deep down in him. All I need is time. Because it's deep down in him.'

The Fusilier was of the opinion that the bird was physically perfect but that some delicate imbalance in its psyche caused it to have momentary blackouts when it was on the wing. All birds, he explained to Judith, depended for their direction on the action of the earth's magnetic grid on the membrane of the mind. It had to do with electricity and electrodes, he said. And when Harry's cock was flying it suffered from 'mental blackouts, like blown fuses,' so that it had to fly blind for periods until the psyche righted itself. Something similar happened to men suffering from shell shock, he believed.

With great peals of laughter, Judith relayed this information to Harry at lunch one Sunday. Ever since his mother had become invalided, he had taken his Sunday meals with her.

'Rubbish!' he said, his tears dropping into the rhubarb pie.

'It sounded great to me,' she said.

'All lies,' he grunted.

'Well, can you explain how your birds know how to make their way home over hundreds of miles?'

'Course I can,' he said. 'It's based on science.'

'Science?'

'Every bird has a microscopic eye,' he said patiently. 'What's the first thing he does when he is liberated? He gets away up into the sky and looks about him. With his two eyes—the kind you and me have—he gets his bearings. But with his microscopic eye—it's buried inside his skull—he sort of takes a photograph of the whole country, like a bloody big map in his head. He knows then exactly where he is and plots his course according.'

'Not a doubt in the world?'

'As simple as if he were running on railway lines.'

'Lucky bird,' said Judith. 'Lucky, lucky bird.'

For a second, he wondered at the tone of her voice. But almost at once she was laughing again and telling him that she had had a letter from Billy in Canada. He had married, got himself a good job, and wanted her to join him.

'With the microscopic eye,' said Harry, 'it's as simple as running on railway lines.'

The All Ireland Open Championship was held on Saturday, August 5th. All birds had to be at the liberating station, Mizen Head, County Cork, by nine o'clock the night before. They would be released the following morning at ten, weather conditions being clement and propitious, as the Post put it.

Major O'Donnell volunteered to take all the Mullaghduff entrants in his beach wagon to Mizen Head on Friday. There were seven local competitors: Joe McSorley's checkered hen; the Major's two yearlings; Patsy Boyle's old grey hen, her daughter, and her granddaughter; and Harry's cock. The Major sent word to Harry that he would call for the cock after lunch.

That morning, Harry was a mass of nerves. He spilled a bucket of maize on the floor of the loft, and when he was down on his hands and knees, gathering it up, he cracked his head on the handle of the door. The birds sensed his anxiety and flew recklessly from side to side, cooing, colliding, squabbling, injuring themselves. All except the blue-grey cock. He stood quietly beneath the trap, now on one foot, now on the other, blinking his eyes, waiting.

Judith came panting up the stairs. 'Harry! Harry, where are you?'

'Up here! In the loft!'

She climbed the remaining stairs. 'The Major's below,' she gasped, 'looking for the basket.'

'He's what? Sure, it's not lunchtime yet!'

'It's almost two o'clock,' she said. 'Come on. Here's the basket. Where's the bird?'

'The bird's not ready. I haven't ringed him yet, and he's not washed, and he has to—'

'Give me,' she said, plucking the rubber band from his hand. 'This is him, isn't it?'

56

'That's—Easy! Easy! Handle him gently!'

She picked up the pigeon, turned him over on his back, and slipped the ring over his left foot.

'Now, give him to me,' said Harry. 'I still have to wash him down.'

'You haven't time,' she said briskly. 'The Major won't wait. Where's the red hen?'

Harry pointed to a nest with a wire-mesh door.

Judith opened the door and put the cock in with the hen. She closed the door again.

The cock spread his wings and arched his neck.

'That's enough,' said Harry. 'Take him out.'

'Leave them!' she said with quiet authority, as if the loft was hers and not his.

The other birds settled on their perches and went suddenly still. The hen got to her feet. The cock began beating the mesh with his wings.

'Quick!' Harry snapped. 'Before it's too late!'

'Leave them,' she said softly, staring at them.

'For God's sake, woman, if you let him go on, he won't come back. He won't race!'

'Leave them,' she said again, in a whisper.

'You'll ruin everything! You don't understand—'

'Leave them!'

The hen squatted on the floor. The cock found his balance.

For a second there was no sound. Then, suddenly, violently, Harry pushed her aside. 'By God, I won't!' he shouted. He flung open the door and grabbed the cock. The whole loft went mad again.

'You don't understand, woman,' he said, thrusting the bird into the basket and talking rapidly to atone for his violence. 'If you let him go on, he would never come back. For God's sake, that's the meaning of the wid-owhood system—to get him to come back. You don't understand these things. They're natural—natural and scientific. Look, he's bustin' to get back to her already!

That's what it means, the widowhood system, d'you see?'

'It's a queer system,' she said in a dreamy way, still staring into the cage.

'Look at him! Searching for her! Sure, it's the most natural thing in the world. Just because he can't get her. But if you were to leave them together for a week, by God, he wouldn't fly the length of himself to join her! Funny, isn't it?'

'The Major's waiting,' she said, turning away from the red hen and going to the top of the stairs.

He lifted the basket and followed her.

The Major took the bird, put it into the back of his beach wagon, and drove off. Harry and she stood together at the edge of the pavement and watched the car disappear round the corner.

'How d'you think it'll do?' he said at last.

She lifted her smooth, round face and looked up at him. 'He's bound to come back to her, isn't he?' she asked.

'He'll come back, all right. But it's the time he does it in that matters to me.'

'But he'll always come back, looking for her?'

'Naturally!'

'Searching for her?'

'Provided you don't let them mate first—like you were just going to do,' he said, laughing.

'I hope you're right, Harry,' she said, her hazel eyes looking at something beyond his face.

He sensed her abstraction, a solemnity in her stillness. 'Come on inside,' he said uneasily, because Judith was strange to him when she was not laughing. 'I want you to put a patch on my head.'

Together they went into the shop.

The following morning was blue and fragile, but by afternoon the sky became overcast and a drizzle of rain glazed the streets and rooftops. Even if the bird were to do the two hundred and eighty-one miles from Mizen

Head in eight hours, Harry calculated—and to beat McSorley's hen it would have to do at least that—it would not arrive back in Mullaghduff until six that evening. But every quarter of an hour after he had made his lunch, he found himself running from the shop to the loft and back again to the shop. Eventually, he closed the shop altogether and joined Handme and the Fusilier in the loft.

He would have been wiser to stay in the shop, because their calm—worse, their assumption that the cock would never make its way back in such weather—unnerved him altogether.

'Ah, well,' sighed Handme. 'It's a lesson to us all. If he had been a hen, now . . .'

'There's no comparison,' said the Fusilier. 'Like greyhounds and whippets.'

'The wind and the rain might do their damnedest on him,' Handme went on, 'but he would make it back to the nest, come hell or high water. Nature is a wonderful invention.'

'But he's a cock,' said the Fusilier.

'A strong cock, not a bad cock at all, but still a cock,' said Handme. The details of the bird's possible loss interested him. 'Would he even have made the length of Limerick?' he asked the Fusilier.

'At the very outside,' said the Fusilier.

'If the north-Cork hawks didn't get him first.'

'Bad brutes, them.'

'They've been known to attack children—even north-Cork children.'

'Or maybe he broke his neck on the telegraph wires.'

'All the same, the spirit would have been game enough.'

'He had spirit; I'll say that for him.'

'And staying power.'

'But a cock,' said the Fusilier.

'A good cock, but still a cock.'

'Give me the natural system every time.'

'That's what's wrong with the widowhood system,' said Handme. 'It's just not natural.'

Harry watched the rain blacken the trunks of the pine trees. 'It's in him,' he muttered. 'It's deep down in him.'

'What's that, Harry?' asked the Fusilier.

Harry turned round. 'Go in next door,' he said, 'and tell Judith to make us a pot of tea. We have a couple of hours to wait yet.'

'And get us some refreshments when you're out!' Handme called after the Fusilier.

'The All Ireland Open must be a wonderful sight,' Handme went on. 'To see five or six thousand birds being liberated at the one time.' He licked his lips and bared his teeth until the gums showed. 'Man, it's something I dream about. A lovely summer morning, and ten thousand fluttering angels rising up to heaven and painting the celestial sky with white and grey and—'

'D'you know what I dream about?' snapped Harry. 'That someday you'll pay me the seven months' rent you owe me!'

Handme lowered his head, and Harry went back to the traps and stared out at the rain. Even the birds went silent, squatting motionless on the perches, watching.

The Fusilier came back with two dozen stout and the news that Judith was not at home.

'Of course she's in. She's always in on a Saturday afternoon,' said Harry.

'I'm telling you she's not,' said the Fusilier. 'Go and see for yourself. Anyhow, the gas man's down there, looking to read your meter.'

Harry saw to the gas man, and then went into Judith's house. It was empty. He went through the narrow hall, into the kitchen, and out to the back garden, calling, 'Judith! Are you home, Judith?' He stood at the bottom of the stairs and called up, 'Judith! Judith?' There was no reply.

Then, for no reason at all except that the race had upset him, the thought suddenly struck him that maybe she was lying dying across the bed. He tore up the stairs and flung open the bedroom door. The room was empty. Only her pink nightdress lay across the bottom of the bed. His calm returned. He came downstairs again, pulled the front door after him, and went back to his own house. Before he went up to the loft, he took a handkerchief from the row that was drying in front of the range in the kitchen, because his eyes were giving him hell.

By the time the bottles were finished, Handme and the Fusilier had discussed politics, the Church, and the decline in public morals. Harry heard them but did not listen. He was battling north with his bird, fighting wind and rain and telegraph poles and hawks. His microscopic eye was not functioning, and he was flying by instinct, doggedly, over wet black bogs and dirty lakes and sodden fields, uncertain if he was going in the right direction but determined to carry on. The terrible effort anaesthetized him; his mind was numb. The labour of keeping his cock aloft and flying and of magnetizing it to himself exhausted him.

'She might,' he heard the Fusilier saying.

'It would be the sensible thing to do,' said Handme.

Dusk was falling. The birds were making their settling-in night noises.

'She's still a strong young woman,' said Handme.

'And they say Canada's a fine country,' said the Fusilier.

'She'll go, all right,' said Handme.

Harry dried his eyes. 'Go where?' he asked. 'Who?'

'I'm just telling the Fusilier here that Judith's thinking of joining the brother in Canada.'

'How do you know that?' said Harry. His mind was stirring again. The exhaustion was melting from his body.

'She was telling me herself.'

'What about a drink, boys?' the Fusilier broke in. 'Do you feel like going out for some, Harry?'

'Yes,' said Harry. 'Yes—Yes, I'll go and get some.'

As he was leaving the loft, Handme was saying, 'With all this automation and stuff, what in God's name will men do with their leisure time? That's what worries me.'

The smirking dummies in Handme's living room leered at Harry as he passed them, and whispered, 'Canada! Canada! Canada!' Their soft, insinuating voices followed him down to the ground floor.

'Like hell!' he said aloud to himself. 'Like bloody hell!' But the sound of his own voice, unechoed, unanswered, only aggravated the fear that was growing in him.

Slowly, controlling his steps, refusing to be panicked, he walked into the house next door.

'Judith!' he called sternly. Then again, 'Judith!'

When no reply came, his fears babbled to him excitedly. 'She's gone to Billy in Canada!' He saw her again as she stood in the loft, watching the cock and the hen. He heard her ask, 'He'll always come back, looking for her?'

He came out into the street and stood in the rain, and again tried to will his frightened mind into silence. But it would not be still. It drove him into motion, moving his legs, slowly at first, then urging him forward more and more quickly, until he was trotting along Distillery Lane and out the Dublin road towards the glove factory. Of course she was not there. It was the half day; the big iron gates were locked. Nor was she in the church. Nor was she anywhere about the three streets that met in the square. And by now his brain had ceased functioning again, although his body was still fresh—even vigorous. If the mind had been capable of throwing up any suggestion, however absurd—she had gone to visit cousins in Letterkenny; she had gone shopping to Coleraine—he would have gone there at once. But his mind was comatose, and only his stupid body kept going, eagerly, pointlessly. Three times he tried the church; three times he went round the square. And then exhausted, he came back to her house again.

The door was open. The smell of frying met him in the hall.

'Judith? Judy?'

'Harry?' her untroubled voice answered from the kitchen.

He closed the door behind him and groped his way through the hall. His tears were blinding him.

From then on, he never knew exactly what happened. Afterwards, he had a vague memory of catching her plump hands in his and kissing them roughly, of her asking him over and over again, 'Are you sober, Harry? Are you sober?' and of her laughter bubbling, swelling, rising to an unnatural pitch, and then stopping altogether. He just closed his eyes and held her while she poured out a flow of gibberish about how that afternoon his talk of the widowhood system had given her the idea of going away, going anywhere, with the certainty at first that he would come searching for her. And then, when she was wandering along the Strabane road, how that certainty abandoned her, and how she had had to come back. He knew that he had tried to answer her, but he could only repeat that he had been running in search of her 'like a bloody pigeon'. He kept saying with incredulity, 'Like a bloody stupid pigeon!'

The only memory of their reunion that would always remain sharp and clear to him was of her whispering to him, at some stage, 'Will you marry me, Harry?' and of himself kissing her on the mouth in love and gratitude, because somehow, at that moment, the question seemed apt. More than apt—inspired.

It was no time to talk of the race, he was aware of that, but that was what he talked of for the next half hour—of the bird's strength and courage and determination; of his confidence that it would make Mullaghduff, maybe not in winning time, but at least completing the course. (And he was right about that, at least; the cock turned up at the loft just after noon the next day.) Talk of the cock led him to Handme and the Fusilier—the big long string and the wee tight keg—sitting in the dusk of the loft, discussing automation, their feet ringed with empty bottles, waiting for replenishments. The more he talked of them, the funnier they seemed to be. Never before had they seemed funny. After all, they were his friends, his best friends. But now, for the first time, he saw them in another way and they were ludicrous—two middle-aged men wasting their lives waiting for a pigeon to come home! He began to chuckle. The chuckle grew into a laugh. In the end, he was laughing so that his sides hurt and his eyes were streaming with water. And in the crook of his arm Judith was laughing, too, and crying, too. And for that half hour, for all the crying, they were the happiest couple in the whole of Mullaghduff.

The Potato Gatherers

November frost had starched the flat countryside into silent rigidity. The 'rat-tat-tat' of the tractor's exhaust drilled into the clean, hard air but did not penetrate it; each staccato sound broke off as if it had been nipped. Hunched over the driver's wheel sat Kelly, the owner, a rock of a man with a huge head and broken fingernails, and in the trailer behind were his four potato gatherers —two young men, permanent farm hands, and the two boys he had hired for the day. At six o'clock in the morning, they were the only living things in that part of County Tyrone.

The boys chatted incessantly. They stood at the front of the trailer, legs apart, hands in their pockets, their faces pressed forward into the icy rush of air, their senses edged for perception. Joe, the elder of the two—he was thirteen and had worked for Kelly on two previous occasions—might have been quieter, but his brother's excitement was infectious. For this was Philly's first job, his first time to take a day off from school to earn money, his first opportunity to prove that he was a man at twelve years of age. His energy was a burden to him. Behind them, on the floor of the trailer, the two farm hands lay sprawled in half sleep.

Twice the boys had to cheer. The first time was when they were passing Dicey O'Donnell's house, and Philly, who was in the same class as Dicey, called across to the thatched, smokeless building, 'Remember me to all the boys, Dicey!' The second time was when they came to the school itself. It was then that Kelly turned to them and growled to them to shut up.

'Do you want the whole county to know you're taking the day off?' he said. 'Save your breath for your work.'

When Kelly faced back to the road ahead, Philly stuck his thumbs in his ears, put out his tongue, and wriggled his fingers at the back of Kelly's head. Then, suddenly forgetting him, he said, 'Tell me, Joe, what are you going to buy?'

'Buy?'

'With the money we get today. I know what I'm getting—a shotgun. Bang! Bang! Bang! Right there, mistah. Jist you put your two hands up above your head and I reckon you'll live a little longer.' He menaced Kelly's neck.

'Agh!' said Joe derisively.

'True as God, Joe. I can get it for seven shillings—an old one that's lying in Tom Tracy's father's barn. Tom told me he would sell it for seven shillings.'

'Who would sell it?'

'Tom.'

'Steal it, you mean. From his old fella.'

'His old fella has a new one. This one's not wanted.' He sighted along an imaginary barrel and picked out an unsuspecting sparrow in the hedge. 'Bang! Never knew what hit you, did you? What are you going to buy, Joe?'

'I don't know. There won't be much to buy with. Maybe—naw, I don't know. Depends on what Ma gives us back.'

'A bicycle. Joe. What about a bike? Quinn would give his away for a packet of cigarettes. You up on the saddle, Joe, and me on the crossbar. Out to the millrace every evening. Me shooting all the rabbits along the way. Bang! Bang! Bang! What about a bike, Joe?'

'I don't know. I don't know.'

'What did she give you back the last time?'

'I can't remember.'

'Ten shillings? More? What did you buy then? A leather belt? A set of rabbit snares?'

'I don't think I got anything back. Maybe a shilling. I don't remember.'

'A shilling! One lousy shilling out of fourteen! Do you know what I'm going to buy?' He hunched his shoulders and lowered his head between them. One eye closed in a huge wink. 'Tell no one? Promise?'

'What?'

'A gaff. See?'

'What about the gun?'

'It can wait until next year. But a gaff, Joe. See? Old Philly down there beside the Black Pool. A big salmon. A beaut. Flat on my belly, and—*phwist!*—there he is on the bank, the gaff stuck in his guts.' He clasped his middle and writhed in agony, imitating the fish. Then his act switched suddenly back to cowboys and he drew from both holsters at a cat sneaking home along the hedge. 'Bang! Bang! That sure settled you, boy. Where *is* this potato territory, mistah? Ah want to show you hombres what work is. What's a-keeping this old tractor-buggy?'

'We're jist about there, Mistah Philly, sir,' said Joe. 'Ah reckon you'll show us, O.K. You'll show us.'

The field was a two-acre rectangle bordered by a low hedge. The ridges of potatoes stretched lengthwise in straight, black lines. Kelly unfastened the trailer and hooked up the mechanical digger. The two labourers stood with their hands in their pockets and scowled around them, cigarettes hanging from their lips.

'You two take the far side,' Kelly told them. 'And Joe, you and—' He could not remember the name. 'You and the lad there, you two take this side. You show him what to do, Joe.' He climbed up on the tractor seat. 'And remember,' he called over his shoulder, 'if the school-attendance officer appears, it's up to you to run. I never seen you. I never heard of you.'

67

The tractor moved forward into the first ridges, throwing up a spray of brown earth behind it as it went.

'Right,' said Joe. 'What we do is this, Philly. When the digger passes, we gather the spuds into these buckets and then carry the buckets to the sacks and fill them. Then back again to fill the buckets. And back to the sacks. O.K., mistah?'

'O.K., mistah. Child's play. What does he want four of us for? I could do the whole field myself—one hand tied behind my back.'

Joe smiled at him. 'Come on, then. Let's see you.'

'Just you watch,' said Philly. He grabbed a bucket and ran stumbling across the broken ground. His small frame bent over the clay and his thin arms worked madly. Before Joe had begun gathering, Philly's voice called to him. 'Joe! Look! Full already! Not bad, eh?'

'Take your time,' Joe called back.

'And look, Joe! Look!' Philly held his hands out for his brother's inspection. They were coated with earth. 'How's that, Joe? They'll soon be as hard as Kelly's!'

Joe laughed. 'Take it easy, Philly. No rush.'

But Philly was already stooped again over his work, and when Joe was emptying his first bucket into the sack, Philly was emptying his third. He gave Joe the huge wink again and raced off.

Kelly turned at the bottom of the field and came back up. Philly was standing waiting for him.

'What you need is a double digger, Mr. Kelly!' he called as the tractor passed. But Kelly's eyes never left the ridges in front of him. A flock of seagulls swooped and dipped behind the tractor, fluttering down to catch worms in the newly turned earth. The boy raced off with his bucket.

'How's it going?' shouted Joe after another twenty minutes. Philly was too busy to answer.

A pale sun appeared about eight-thirty. It was not strong enough to soften the earth, but it loosened sounds —cars along the road, birds in the naked trees, cattle let out for the day. The clay became damp under it but did not thaw. The tractor exulted in its new freedom and its splutterings filled the countryside.

'I've been thinking,' said Philly when he met Joe at a sack. 'Do you know what I'm going to get, Joe? A scout knife with one of those leather scabbards. Four shillings in Byrne's shop. Great for skinning a rabbit.' He held his hands out from his sides now, because they were raw in places. 'Yeah. A scout knife with a leather scabbard.'

'A scout knife,' Joe repeated.

'You always have to carry a scout knife in case your gun won't fire or your powder gets wet. And when you're swimming underwater, you can always carry a knife between your teeth.'

'We'll have near twenty ridges done before noon,' said Joe.

'He should have a double digger. I told him that. Too slow, mistah. Too doggone slow. Tell me, Joe, have you made up your mind yet?'

'What about?'

'What you're going to buy, stupid.'

'Aw, naw. Naw . . . I don't know yet.'

Philly turned to his work again and was about to begin, when the school bell rang. He dropped his bucket and danced back to his brother. 'Listen! Joe! Listen!' He caught fistfuls of his hair and tugged his head from side to side. 'Listen! Listen! Ha, ha, ha! Ho, ho, ho! Come on, you fat, silly, silly scholars and get to your lessons! Come on, come on, come on, come on! No dallying! Speed it up! Get a move on! Hurry! Hurry! Hurry! "And where are the O'Boyle brothers today? Eh? Where are they? Gathering potatoes? What's that I hear? What? What?" '

'Look out, lad!' roared Kelly.

The tractor passed within inches of Philly's legs. He jumped out of its way in time, but a fountain of clay fell on his head and shoulders. Joe ran to his side.

'Are you all right, Philly? Are you O.K.?'

'Tried to get me, that's what he did, the dirty cattle thief. Tried to get me.'

'You O.K., mistah? Reckon you'll live?'

'Sure, mistah. Take more'n that ole coyote to scare me. Come on, mistah. We'll show him what men we really are.' He shook his jacket and hair and hitched up his trousers. 'Would you swap now, Joe?'

'Swap what?'

'Swap places with those poor eejits back there?' He jerked his thumb in the direction of the school.

'No sir,' said Joe. 'Not me.'

'Nor me neither, mistah. Meet you in the saloon.' He swaggered off, holding his hands as if they were delicate things, not part of him.

They broke off for lunch at noon. By then, the sun was high and brave but still of little use. With the engine of the tractor cut off, for a brief time there was a self-conscious silence, which became relaxed and natural when the sparrows, now audible, began to chirp. The seagulls squabbled over the latest turned earth and a cautious puff of wind stirred the branches of the tall trees. Kelly adjusted the digger while he ate. On the far side of the field, the two labourers stretched themselves on sacks and conversed in monosyllables. Joe and Philly sat on upturned buckets. For lunch they each had half a scone of homemade soda bread, cut into thick slices and skimmed with butter. They washed it down with mouthfuls of cold tea from a bottle. After they had eaten, Joe threw the crusts to the gulls, gathered up the newspapers in which the bread had been wrapped, emptied out the remains of the tea, and put the bottle and the papers into his jacket pocket. Then he stood up and stretched himself.

'My back's getting stiff,' he said.

Philly sat with his elbows on his knees and studied the palms of his hands.

'Sore?' asked Joe.

'What?'

'Your hands. Are they hurting you?'

'They're O.K.,' said Philly. 'Tough as leather. But the clay's sore. Gets right into every cut and away up your nails.' He held his arms out. 'They're shaking,' he said. 'Look.'

'That's the way they go,' said Joe. 'But they'll—Listen! Do you hear?'

'Hear what?'

'Lunchtime at school. They must be playing football in the playground.'

The sounds of high, delighted squealing came intermittently when the wind sighed. They listened to it with their heads uplifted, their faces broadening with memory.

'We'll get a hammering tomorrow,' said Joe. 'Six on each hand.'

'It's going to be a scout knife,' Philly said. 'I've decided on that.'

'She mightn't give us anything back. Depends on how much she needs herself.'

'She said she would. She promised. Have you decided yet?'

'I'm still thinking,' said Joe.

The tractor roared suddenly, scattering every other sound.

'Come on, mistah,' said the older one. 'Four more hours to go. Saddle up your horse.'

'Coming. Coming,' Philly replied. His voice was sharp with irritation.

The sun was a failure. It held its position in the sky and flooded the countryside with light but could not warm it. Even before it had begun to slip to the west, the damp ground had become glossy again, and before the afternoon was spent, patches of white frost were appearing on higher ground. Now the boys were working automatically, their minds acquiescing in what their bodies did. They no longer straightened up; the world was their feet and the hard clay and the potatoes and their hands and the buckets and the sacks. Their ears told them where the tractor was, at the bottom of the field, turning, approaching. Their muscles had become adjusted to their stooped position, and as long as the boys kept within the established pattern of movement their arms and hands and legs and shoulders seemed to float as if they were free of gravity. But if something new was expected from the limbs—a piece of glass to be thrown in to the hedge, a quick stepping back to avoid the digger—then their bodies shuddered with pain and the tall trees reeled and the hedges rose to the sky.

Dicey O'Donnell gave them a shout from the road on his way home from school. 'Hi! Joe! Philly!'

They did not hear him. He waited until the tractor turned. 'Hi! Hi! Philly! Philly! Joe! Youse are for it the morrow. I'm telling youse. He knows where youse are. He says he's going to beat the scruff out of youse the morrow. Youse are in for it, all right. Blue murder! Bloody hell! True as God!'

'Get lost!' Joe called back.

'Aye, and he's going to report youse to the attendance officer, and your old fella'll be fined. Youse are ruined! Destroyed! Blue murder!'

'Will I put a bullet in him, mistah?' said Joe to Philly.

Philly did not answer. He thought he was going to fall, and his greatest fear was that he might fall in front of the tractor, because now the tractor's exhaust had only one sound, fixed forever in his head, and unless he saw the machine he could not tell whether it was near him or far away. The 'rat-tat-tat' was a finger tapping in his head, drumming at the back of his eyes.

'Vamoose, O'Donnell!' called Joe. 'You annoy us. Vamoose.'

O'Donnell said something more about the reception they could expect the next day, but he got tired of calling to two stooped backs and he went off home.

The last pair of ridges was turned when the sky had veiled itself for dusk. The two brothers and the two labourers worked on until they met in the middle. Now the field was all brown, all flat, except for the filled sacks that patterned it. Kelly was satisfied; his lips formed an O and he blew through them as if he were trying to whistle. He detached the digger and hooked up the trailer. 'All aboard!' he shouted, in an effort at levity.

On the way home, the labourers seemed to be fully awake, for the first time since morning. They stood in the trailer where the boys had stood at dawn, behind Kelly's head and facing the road before them. They chatted and guffawed and made plans for a dance that night. When they met people they knew along the way, they saluted extravagantly. At the crossroads, they began to wrestle, and Kelly had to tell them to watch out or they would fall over the side. But he did not sound angry.

Joe sat on the floor, his legs straight out before him, his back resting against the side of the trailer. Philly lay flat out, his head cushioned on his brother's lap. Above him, the sky spread out, grey, motionless, enigmatic. The warmth from Joe's body made him drowsy. He wished the journey home to go on forever, the sound of the tractor engine to anaesthetize his mind forever. He knew that if the movement and the sound were to cease, the pain of his body would be unbearable.

'We're nearly there,' said Joe quietly. 'Are you asleep?' Philly did not answer. 'Mistah! Are you asleep, mistah?'

'No.'

Darkness came quickly, and when the last trace of light disappeared the countryside became taut with frost. The headlamps of the tractor glowed yellow in the cold air.

'Philly? Are you awake, mistah?'

'What?'

'I've been thinking,' said Joe slowly. 'And do you know what I think? I think I've made up my mind now.'

One of the labourers burst into song.

73

'"If I were a blackbird, I'd whistle and sing, and I'd follow the ship that my true love sails in."'

His mate joined him at the second line and their voices exploded in the stiff night.

'Do you know what I'm going to buy?' Joe said, speaking more loudly. 'If she gives us something back, that is. Mistah! Mistah Philly! Are you listening? I'm going to buy a pair of red silk socks.'

He waited for approval from Philly. When none came, he shook his brother's head. 'Do you hear, mistah? Red silk socks—the kind Jojo Teague wears. What about that, eh? What do you think?'

Philly stirred and half raised his head from his brother's lap. 'I think you're daft,' he said in an exhausted, sullen voice. 'Ma won't give us back enough to buy anything much. No more than a shilling. You knew it all the time.' He lay down again and in a moment he was fast asleep.

Joe held his brother's head against the motion of the trailer and repeated the words 'red silk socks' to himself again and again, nodding each time at the wisdom of his decision.

Foundry House

When his father and mother died, Joe Brennan applied for their house, his old home, the gate lodge to Foundry House. He wrote direct to Mr. Bernard (as Mr. Hogan was known locally), pointing out that he was a radio-and-television mechanic in the Music Shop; that although he had never worked for Mr. Hogan, his father had been an employee in the foundry for over fifty years; and that he himself had been born and reared in the gate lodge. Rita, his wife, who was more practical than he, insisted that he mention their nine children and the fact that they were living in three rooms above a launderette.

'That should influence him,' she said. 'Aren't they supposed to be one of the best Catholic families in the North of Ireland?' So, against his wishes, he added a paragraph about his family and their inadequate accommodation, and sent off his application. Two days later, he received a reply from Mrs. Hogan, written on mauve scented notepaper with fluted edges. Of course she remembered him, she said. He was the small, round-faced boy with the brown curls who used to play with her Declan. And to think that he now had nine babies of his own! Where did time go? He could collect the keys from the agent and move in as soon as he wished. There were no longer any duties attached to the position of gatekeeper, she added—not since wartime, when the authorities had taken away the great iron gates that sealed the mouth of the avenue.

'Brown curls!' Rita squealed with delight when Joe read her the letter. 'Brown curls! She mustn't have seen you for twenty years or more!'

'That's all right now,' was all Joe could say. He was moved with relief and an odd sense of humility at his unworthiness. 'That's all right. That's all right.'

They moved into their new house at the end of summer. It was a low-set, solid stone building with a steep roof and exaggerated eaves that gave it the appearance of a gnome's house in a fairy tale. The main Derry-Belfast road ran parallel to the house, and on the other side the ground rose rapidly in a tangle of shrubs and wild rhododendron and decaying trees, through which the avenue crawled up to Foundry House at the top of the hill. The residence was not visible from the road or from any part of the town; one could only guess at its location somewhere in the green patch that lay between the new housing estate and the brassière factory. But Joe remembered from his childhood that if one stood at the door of Foundry House on a clear morning, before the smoke from the red-brick factories clouded the air, one could see through the trees and the undergrowth, past the gate lodge and the busy main road, and right down to the river below, from which the sun drew a million momentary flashes of light that danced and died in the vegetation.

For Joe, moving into the gate lodge was a homecoming; for Rita and the children, it was a changeover to a new life. There were many improvements to be made —there was no indoor toilet and no running water, the house was lit by gas only, and the windows, each made up a score of small, diamond-shaped pieces of glass, gave little light—and Joe accepted that they were inevitable. But he found himself putting them off from day to day and from week to week. He did not have much time when he came home from work, because the evenings were getting so short. Also, he had applied to the urban council for a money grant, and they were sending along an architect soon. And he had to keep an eye on the children, who looked on the grounds as their own private park and climbed trees and lit fires in the undergrowth and played their shrieking games of hide-and-seek or cowboys-and-Indians right up to the very front of the big house itself.

'Come back here! Come back!' Joe would call after them in an urgent undertone. 'Why can't you play down below near your own house? Get away down at once with you!'

'We want to play up here, Daddy,' some of them would plead. 'There are better hiding places up here.'

'The old man, he'll soon scatter you!' Joe would say. 'Or he'll put the big dog on you. God help you then!'

'But there is no old man. Only the old woman and the maid. And there is no dog, either.'

'No Mr. Bernard? Huh! Just let him catch you, and you'll know all about it. No Mr. Bernard! The dog may be gone, but Mr. Bernard's not. Come on now! Play around your own door or else come into the house altogether.'

No Mr. Bernard! Mr. Bernard always had been, Joe thought to himself, and always would be—a large, stern-faced man with a long white beard and a heavy step and a walking stick, the same ever since he remembered him. And beside him the Great Dane, who copied his master as best he could in expression and gait—a dour, sullen animal as big as a calf and as savage as a tiger, according to the men in the foundry. And Mrs. Hogan? He supposed she could be called an old woman now, too. Well over sixty, because Declan and he were of an age, and he was thirty-three himself. Yes, an old woman, or at least elderly, even though she was twenty years younger than her husband. And not Declan now, or even Master Declan, but Father Declan, a Jesuit. And then there was Claire, Miss Claire, the girl, younger than Declan by a year. Fat, blue-eyed Claire, who had blushed every time she passed the gate lodge because she knew some of the Brennans were sure to be peering out through the diamond windows. She had walked with her head to one side, as if she were listening for something, and used to trail her fingers along the boxwood that fringed both sides of the avenue. 'Such a lovely girl,' Joe's mother used to say. 'So simple and so sweet. Not like the things I see running about this town. There's something good before that child. Something very good.' And she was right. Miss Claire was now Sister Claire of the Annuciation Nuns and was out in Africa. Nor would she ever be home again. Never. Sister Claire and Father Declan—just the two of them, and both of them in religion, and the big house up above going to pieces, and no one to take over the foundry when the time would come. Everything they could want in the world, anything that money could buy, and they turned their backs on it all. Strange, Joe thought. Strange. But right, because they were the Hogans.

They were a month in the house and were seated at their tea, all eleven of them, when Mrs. Hogan called on them. It was now October and there were no evenings to speak of; the rich, warm days ended abruptly in a dusk that was uneasy with cold breezes. Rita was relieved at the change in the weather, because now the children, still unsure of the impenetrable dark and the nervous movements in the undergrowth, were content to finish their games when daylight failed, and she had no difficulty in gathering them for their evening meal. Joe answered the knock at the door.

'I'm so sorry to disturb you, Mr. Brennan. But I wonder could you do me a favour?'

She was a tall, ungraceful woman, with a man's shoulders and a wasted body and long, thin feet. When she spoke, her mouth and lips worked in excessive movement.

Rita was at Joe's elbow. 'Did you not ask the woman in?' she reproved him. 'Come on inside, Mrs. Hogan.'

'I'm sorry,' Joe stammered. 'I thought . . . I was about to . . .' How could he say he didn't dare?

'Thank you all the same,' Mrs. Hogan said. 'But I oughtn't to have left Bernard at all. What brought me down was this. Mary—our maid, you know—she tells me that you have a tape-recording machine. She says you're in that business. I wonder could we borrow it for an afternoon? Next Sunday?'

'Certainly, Mrs. Hogan. Certainly,' said Rita. 'Take it with you now. We never use it. Do we, Joe?'

'If Sunday suits you, I would like to have it then when Father Declan comes,' Mrs. Hogan said. 'You see, my daughter, Claire, has sent us a tape-recording of her voice—these nuns nowadays, they're so modern—and we were hoping to have Father Declan with us when we play it. You know, a sort of family reunion, on Sunday.'

'Any time at all,' said Rita. 'Take it with you now. Go and get it, Joe, and carry it up.'

'No, no. Really. Sunday will do—Sunday afternoon. Besides, neither Bernard nor I know how to work the machine. We'll be depending on you to operate it for us, Mr. Brennan.'

'And why wouldn't he?' said Rita. 'He does nothing on a Sunday afternoon, anyway. Certainly he will.'

Now that her request had been made and granted, Mrs. Hogan stood irresolutely between the white gas-light in the hall and the blackness outside. Her mouth and lips still worked, although no sound came.

'Sunday then,' she said at last. 'A reunion.'

'Sunday afternoon,' said Rita. 'I'll send him up as soon as he has his dinner in him.'

'Thank you,' said Mrs. Hogan. 'Thank you.' Her mouth formed an O, and she drew in her breath. But she snapped it shut again and turned and strode off up the avenue.

Rita closed the door and leaned against it. She doubled up with laughter. 'Lord, if you could only see your face!' she gasped between bursts.

'What do you mean, my face?'

'All scared-looking, like a child caught stealing!'

'What are you raving about?' he asked irritably.

'And she was as scared-looking as yourself.' She held her hand to her side. 'She must have been looking for the brown curls and the round face! And not a word out of you! Like a big, scared dummy!'

'Shut up,' he mumbled gruffly. 'Shut up, will you?'

Joe had never been inside Foundry House, had never spoken to Mr. Bernard, and had not seen Declan since his Ordination. And now, as he stood before the hall door and the evil face on the leering knocker, the only introductory remark his mind would supply him was one from his childhood: 'My daddy says here are the keys to the workshop and that he put out the fire in the office before he left.' He was still struggling to suppress this senseless memory when Father Declan opened the door.

'Ah, Joe, Joe, Joe! Come inside. Come inside. We are waiting for you. And you have the machine with you? Good man! Good man! Great! Great!'

Father Declan was fair and slight, and his gestures fluttering and birdlike. The black suit accentuated the whiteness of his hair and skin and hands.

'Straight ahead, Joe. First door to the right. You know—the breakfast room. They live there now, Father and Mother. Convenient to the kitchen, and all. And Mother tells me you are married and have a large family?'

'That's right, Father.'

'Good man! Good man! Marvellous, too. No, no, not that door, Joe, the next one. No, they don't use the drawing room any more. Too large and too expensive to heat. That's it, yes. No, no, don't knock. Just go right in. That's it. Good man! Good man!'

One minute he was behind Joe, steering him through the hallway, and the next he had sped past him and was standing in the middle of the floor of the breakfast room, his glasses flashing, his arms extended in reception. 'Good man. Here we are. Joe Brennan, Mother, with the tape recorder.'

'So kind of you, Joe,' said Mrs. Hogan, emerging from behind the door. 'It's going to be quite a renunion, isn't it?'

'How many young Brennans are there?' asked Father Declan.

'Nine, Father.'

'Good! Good! Great! Great!'

'Such healthy childhen too,' said Mrs. Hogan. 'I've seen them playing on the avenue. And so . . . so healthy.'

'Have a seat, Joe. Just leave the recorder there. Anywhere at all. Good man. That's it. Fine!'

'You've had your lunch, Mr. Brennan?'

'Yes, thanks, Mrs. Hogan. Thank you all the same.'

'What I mean is, you didn't rush off without it?'

'Lucky for you, Joe,' the priest broke in. 'Because these people, I discover, live on snacks now. Milk and bananas—that sort of thing.'

'You'll find the room cold, I'm afraid, Mr. Brennan.'

'If you have a power plug. I'll get this thing . . .'

'A power plug. A power plug. A power plug. A power plug.' The priest cracked his fingers each time he said the words and frowned in concentration.

'What about that thing there?' asked Mrs. Hogan, pointing to the side of the mantelpiece.

'That's a gas bracket, Mother. No. Electric. Electric.' One white finger rested on his chin. 'An electric power plug. There must be one somewhere in the—ah! Here we are!' He dropped on his knees below the window and looked back exultantly over his shoulder. 'I just thought so. Here we are. I knew there must be one somewhere.'

'Did you find one?' asked Mrs. Hogan.

'Yes, we did, didn't we, Joe? Will this do? Does your machine fit this?'

'That's grand, Father.'

81

'Good! Good! Then I'll go and bring Father down. He's in bed resting. Where is the tape, Mother?'

'Tape? Oh, the tape! Yes, there on the sideboard.'

'Fine! Fine! That's everything then. Father and I will be down in a minute. Good! Good!'

'Logs,' said Mrs. Hogan to herself. Then, remembering Joe, she said to him, 'We burn our own fuel. For economy.' She smiled bleakly at him and followed her son from the room.

Joe busied himself with rigging up the machine and putting the new tape in position. When he was working in someone's house, it was part of his routine to examine the pictures and photographs around the walls, to open drawers and presses, to finger ornaments and bric-à-brac. But, here in Foundry House, a modesty, a shyness, a vague deference to something long ago did not allow his eyes even to roam from the work he was engaged in. Yet he was conscious of certain aspects of the room; the ceiling was high, perhaps as high as the roof of his own house, the fireplace was of black marble, the door handle was of cut glass, and the door itself did not close properly. Above his head was a print of horses galloping across open fields; the corner of the carpet was nibbled away. His work gave him assurance.

'There you are now, Mrs. Hogan,' he said when she returned with a big basket of logs. 'All you have to do is turn this knob and away she goes.'

She ignored his stiff movement to help her with her load of logs, and knelt at the fireplace until she had built up the fire. Then, rubbing her hands down her skirt, she came and stood beside him.

'What was that, Mr. Brennan?'

'I was saying that all you have to do is to turn this knob here to start it going, and turn it back to stop it. Nothing at all to it.'

'Yes?' she said, thrusting her lips forward, her mind a blank.

'That's all,' said Joe. 'Right to start, left to stop. A child could work it.' He tugged at the lapels of his jacket to indicate that he was ready to leave.

'No difficulty at all,' she repeated dreamily. Then suddenly alert again, 'Here they come. You sit there, Mr. Brennan, on this side of the fire, Father Declan will sit here, and I will sit beside the table. A real family circle.'

'You'll want to listen to this by yourselves, Mrs. Hogan. So if you don't mind . . .'

'Don't leave, Mr. Brennan. You will stay, won't you? You remember Claire, our lovely Claire. You remember her, don't you? She's out in Africa, you know, and she'll never be home again. Never. Not even for a death. You'll stay, and hear her talking to us, won't you? Of course you will.' Her finger tips touched the tops of her ears. 'Claire's voice again. Talking to us. And you'll want to hear it too, won't you?'

Before he could answer, the door burst open. Mr. Bernard had come down.

It took them five minutes to get from the door to the leather armchair beside the fire, and Joe was reminded of a baby being taught to walk. Father Declan came in first, backward, crouching slightly, his eyes on his father's feet and his arms outstretched and beckoning. 'Slow-ly. Slow-ly,' he said in a hypnotist's voice. 'Slow-ly. Slow-ly.' Then his father appeared. First a stick, then a hand, an arm, the curve of his stomach, then the beard, yellow and untidy, then the whole man. Since his return to the gate lodge, Joe had not thought of Mr. Bernard beyond the fact that he was there. In his mind there was a twenty-year-old image that had never been adjusted, a picture which was so familiar to him that he had long since ceased to look at it. But this was not the image, this giant who had grown in height and swollen in girth instead of shrinking, this huge, monolithic figure that inched its way across the faded carpet, one mechanical step after the other, in response to a word from the black, weaving figure before him. Joe looked at his face, fleshy, trembling, coloured in dead purple and grey-black, and at the eyes, wide and staring and quick with the terror of stumbling or of falling or even of missing a syllable of the instructions from the priest. 'Lift again. Lift it. Lift it. Good. Good. Now down, down. And the right, up and up and up—yes —and now down.' The old man wore an overcoat streaked down the front with food stains, and the hands, one clutching the head of the stick, the other limp and lifeless by his side, were so big they had no contour. His breathing was a succession of rapid sighs.

Until the journey from door to armchair was completed, Mrs. Hogan made fussy jobs for herself and addressed herself to no one in particular. 'The leaves are terrible this year. Simply terrible. I must get a man to sweep them up and do something with the rockery, too, because it has got out of hand altogether . . .'

'Slow-ly. Slow-ly. Left. Left. That's it . . . up yes. Yes. And down again. Down.'

'I never saw such a year for leaves. And the worst of it is the wind just blows them straight up against the hall door. Only this morning, I was saying to Mary we must make a pile of them and burn them before they smother us altogether. A bonfire—that's what we'll make.'

'Now turn. Turn. Turn. That's it. Right round. Round. Round. Now back. Good. Good.'

'Your children would enjoy a bonfire, wouldn't they, Mr. Brennan? Such lively children they are too, and so healthy, so full of life. I see them, you know, from my bedroom window. Running all over the place. So lively and full of spirits.'

A crunch, a heavy thud, and Mr. Bernard was seated, not upright but sideways over the arm of the chair, as he had dropped. His eyes blinked in relief at having missed disaster once more.

'Now,' said Mrs. Hogan briskly, 'I think we're ready to begin, aren't we? This is Mr. Brennan of the gate lodge, Daddy. He has given us the loan of his tape-recording machine and is going to work it for us. Isn't that kind of him?'

'How are you, Mr. Hogan?' said Joe.

The old man did not answer, but looked across at him. Was it a sly, reproving look, Joe wondered, or was it the awkward angle of the old man's head that made it appear sly?

'Which of these knobs is it?' asked Father Declan, his fingers playing arpeggios over the recorder. 'On. This is it, isn't it? Yes. This is it.'

'The second one is for volume, Father,' said Joe.

'Volume. Yes. I see. Well, all set?'

'Ready,' said Mrs. Hogan.

'Ready, Daddy?' asked Father Declan.

'Daddy's ready,' said Mrs. Hogan.

'Joe?'

'Ready,' said Joe, because that was what Mrs. Hogan had said.

'Here goes then,' said Father Declan. 'Come in, Claire. We're waiting.'

The recorder purred. The soft sound of the revolving spools spread up and out until it was heavy as the noise of distant seas. Mrs. Hogan sat at the edge of her chair; Mr. Bernard remained slumped as he had fallen. Father Declan stood poised as a ballet dancer before the fire. The spools gathered speed and the purring was a pounding of blood in the ears.

'It often takes a few seconds—' Joe began.

'Quiet!' snapped Mrs. Hogan. 'Quiet, boy! Quiet!'

Then the voice came and all other sound died.

'Hello, Mammy and Daddy and Father Declan. This is Sister Claire speaking to the three of you from St. Joseph's Mission, Kaluga, Northern Rhodesia. I hope you are all together when this is being played back, because I am imagining you all sitting before a great big fire in the drawing room at this minute, Daddy spread out and taking his well-earned relaxation on one side, and you, Mammy, sitting on the other side, and Declan between you both. How are you all? I wish to talk to each of you in turn—to Declan first, then to you, Mammy, and last, but by no means least, to my dear Daddy. Later in the recording, Reverend Mother, who is here beside me, will say a few words to you, and after that you will hear my school choir singing some Irish songs that I have taught them and some native songs they have taught me. I hope you will enjoy them.'

Joe tried to remember the voice. Then he realized that he probably had never heard Claire speak. This sounded more like reading than speaking, he thought—like a teacher reading a story to a class of infants, making her voice go up and down in pretended interest.

She addressed the priest first, and Joe looked at him—eyes closed, hands joined at the left shoulder, head to the side, feet crossed, his whole body limp and graceful as if in repose. She asked him for his prayers and thanked him for his letter last Christmas. She said that every day she got her children to pray both for him and for the success of his work, and asked him to send her the collection of Irish melodies—a blue-backed book, she said, which he would find either in the piano stool or in the glass bookcase beside the drawing-room window.

'And now you, Mammy. You did not mention your lumbago in your last letter, so I take it you are not suffering so much from it. And I hope you have found a good maid at last, because the house is much too big for you to manage all by yourself. There are many young girls around the mission here who would willingly give you a hand, but then they are too far away, aren't they? However, please God, you are now fixed up.'

She went on to ask about the garden and the summer crop of flowers, and told of the garden she had beside the convent and of the flowers she was growing. While her daughter spoke to her, Mrs. Hogan worked her mouth and lips furiously, and Joe wondered what she was saying to herself.

'And now I come to my own Daddy. How are you, Daddy? I am sure you were very sorry when Prince had to be shot, you had him so long. And then the Prince before that—how long did you have him? I was telling Sister Monica here about him the other day, about the first Prince, and when I said he lived to be nineteen and a half, she just laughed in my face and said she was sure I was mistaken. But he was nineteen and a half, wasn't he? You got him on my sixth birthday, I remember, and although I never saw the second Prince—you got him after I had entered—I am quite sure he was as lovely as the first. Now, why don't you get yourself a third, Daddy? He would be company for you when you go on your rambles, and it would be nice for *you* to have him lying beside you on the office floor, the way the first Prince used to lie.'

Joe watched the old man. Mr. Bernard could not move himself to face the recorder, but his eyes were on it, the large, startled eyes of a horse.

'And now, Daddy, before I talk any more to you, I am going to play a tune for you on my violin. I hope you like it. It is *The Gartan Mother's Lullaby*. Do you remember it?'

She began to play. The music was tuneful but no more. The lean tinny notes found a weakness in the tape or in the machine, because when she played the higher part of the melody, the only sound reproduced was a shrieking monotone. Joe sprang to his feet and worked at the controls but he could do nothing. The sound adjusted itself when she came to the initial melody again, and he went back to his seat.

It was then, as he turned to go back to the fire, that he noticed the old man. He had moved somehow in his armchair and was facing the recorder, staring at it. His one good hand pressed down on the sides of his chair and his body rocked backward and forward. His expression, too, had changed. The dead purple of his cheeks was now a living scarlet, and the mouth was open. Then, even as Joe watched, he suddenly levered himself upright in the chair, his face pulsating with uncontrollable emotion, the veins in his neck dilating, the mouth shaping in preparation for speech. He leaned forward, half pointing towards the recorder with one huge hand.

'Claire!'

The terrible cry—hoarse, breathy, almost lost in his asthmatic snortings—released Father Declan and Mrs. Hogan from their concentration on the tape. They ran to him as he fell back into the chair.

Darkness had fallen by the time Joe left Foundry House. He had helped Father Declan to carry the old man upstairs to his bedroom and helped to undress him and put him to bed. He suggested a doctor, but neither the priest nor Mrs. Hogan answered him. Then he came downstairs alone and switched off the humming machine. He waited for almost an hour for the others to come down—he felt awkward about leaving without making some sort of farewell—but when neither of them came, he tiptoed out through the hall and pulled the door after him. He left the recorder behind.

The kitchen at home was chaotic. The baby was in a zinc bath before the fire, three younger children were wrestling in their pyjamas, and the five elder were eating at the table. Rita, her hair in a turban and her sleeves rolled up, stood in the middle of the floor and shouted unheeded instructions above the din. Joe's arrival drew her temper to him.

'So you came back home at last! Did you have a nice afternoon with your fancy friends?'

He picked his steps between the wrestlers and sat in the corner below the humming gas jet.

'I'm speaking to you! Are you deaf?'

'I heard you,' he said. 'Yes, I had a nice afternoon.'

She sat resolutely on the opposite side of the fireplace, to show that she had done her share of the work; it was now his turn to give a hand.

'Well?' She took a cigarette from her apron pocket and lit it. The chaos around her was forgotten.

'Well, what?' he asked.

'You went up with the recorder, and what happened?'

'They were all there—the three of them.'

'Then what?'

'We played the tape through.'

'What's the house like inside?'

'It's very nice,' Joe said slowly. 'Very nice.'

She waited for him to continue. When he did not, she said, 'Did the grandeur up there frighten you, or what?'

'I was just thinking about them, that's all,' he said.

'The old man, what's he like?'

'Mr. Bernard? Oh, Mr. Bernard . . . he's the same as ever. Older, of course, but the same Mr. Bernard.'

'And Father Declan?'

'A fine man. A fine priest. Yes, very fine.'

'Huh!' said Rita. 'It's not worth your while going out, for all the news you bring home.'

'The tape was lovely,' said Joe quickly. 'She spoke to all of them in turn—to Father Declan and then to her mother and then to Mr. Bernard himself. And she played a tune on the violin for him, too.'

'Did they like it?'

'They loved it, loved it. It was a lovely recording.'

'Did she offer you anything?'

'Forced me to have tea with them, but I said no, I had to leave.'

'What room were they in?'

'The breakfast room. The drawing room was always draughty.'

'A nice room?'

'The breakfast room? Oh, lovely, lovely . . . Glass handle on the door and a beautiful carpet and beautiful pictures . . . everything. Just lovely.'

'So that's Foundry House,' said Rita, knowing that she was going to hear no gossipy details.

'That's Foundry House,' Joe echoed. 'The same as

ever—no different.'

She put out her cigarette and stuck the butt behind her ear.

'They're a great family, Rita,' he said. 'A great, grand family.'

'So they are,' she said casually, stooping to lift the baby out of the bath. Its wet hands patterned her thin blouse. 'Here, Joe! A job for you. Dress this divil for bed.'

She set the baby on his knee and went to separate the wrestlers. Joe caught the child, closed his eyes, and rubbed his cheek against the infant's soft, damp skin. 'The same as ever,' he crooned into the child's ear. 'A great family. A grand family.'

The Illusionists

The annual visit of M. L'Estrange to our school in the first week of March marked the end of winter and the beginning of spring. The bleak countryside around Beannafreaghan was cold-dead when he arrived and perhaps for a few weeks after he had gone, but when we heard the scrape of his handlebars against the school wall and saw his battered silk hat pass the classroom window, the terrible boredom of winter suddenly seemed to vanish, and we knew that good times were imminent.

We hadn't many visitors to Beannafreaghan Primary School where my father was principal and entire staff. Once a month Father Shiels, the manager, drove out the twisted five miles from the town, in one breath asked us were we good and told us to say our prayers, shook father's hand firmly, and scuttled away again as if there were someone chasing him. Occasionally an inspector would come, and father would show him the seeping walls and the cracked windows and the rotting floor, and the inspector would grunt sympathetically and nod his head sadly from side to side and leave without asking us anything. An odd time a salesman for books would come, but no one ever bought anything. And one morning a travelling theatre for schools, a great coloured caravan towed by a landrover, stopped at our gate, and a man with a beard and an English accent breezed in to the classroom. I distinctly overheard father telling him that unfortunately it would be impossible to put on a

91

play that day because the recording unit of the B.B.C. was coming that very afternoon to make choral and verse-speaking tapes. The whole story, of course, was a fabrication: there wasn't a note or a line of verse in any of us. The truth of the matter was that his twenty-five pupils could not afford to pay sixpence a head, not to talk of two-and-six, not even to see an international cast doing international plays.

I never knew which I liked better: to be playing in the school-yard at lunch-time, and look up, and suddenly see the tall figure of M. L'Estrange mounted on his bicycle and free-wheeling recklessly down the long hill that hid us from the town of Omagh; or to be in class, staring dreamily at an open book, and then to hear the scrape of his handlebars against the school wall. I think I preferred him to walk in on us when we were in the middle of lessons, to see the door opening, to hear his deep, resonant voice boom out, 'Am I interrupting the progress of knowledge?' because then the delight was so acute that the mouth dropped open, and the eyes stared, and the heart raced, because there he was, M. L'Estrange, The Illusionist, back again to perform his magic on us. To us rustic children he was the most wonderful man in the world.

Father was stiffly polite to the manager and over-anxious with inspectors but he welcomed M. L'Estrange warmly and enthusiastically. Mother's attitude to the illusionist was at least consistent—she treated him quietly and with caution. But I could never understand father's attitude. There was no doubt that he was delighted to see him. He put his arm round his shoulder, and pumped his hand, and kept looking at us to find a match for his heartiness in our faces (perhaps he mistook our stillness for indifference). But as the afternoon went on, his exuberance quickly evaporated, and he became irritable again, and by the time M. L'Estrange left our house to cycle back to town—always late in the evening, and by then father and he were more than half-drunk

—father had begun taunting him about being nothing more than a trick-of-the-loop man and scarcely better than a tramp. But when he first arrived you would think father had found a long-lost brother. He would exclaim, 'Look, children! Look who's here! M. L'Estrange! Back again!' As if there was any need to tell us to look. Because the moment he appeared in the doorway our quick, country eyes devoured him: the calm face; and the slender white hands; and the long silvery hair that had given a gloss to the collar of his frock-coat; and the black striped trousers, frayed at the bottom; and the soiled white scarf; and the glittering rings. And then, long before I had finished gazing at him, father would send me across the fields to the house to tell mother to have a meal ready for M. L'Estrange after the performance. That was a job I hated doing. Mother never shared my excitement—'Don't tell me that old trickster's here again!'—and by the time I got back the show was ready to begin. It was little consolation to me that, later in the evening when all the other pupils had dispersed, I would have M. L'Estrange all to myself in my own house. What happened was that invariably I missed the preparations: the clearing of father's table; M. L'Estrange putting on his black mask; the hanging of the curtain between the black-board and the fireplace; the arranging of the desks in three rows. The smallest children, frozen with delicious nervousness, sat in the front seats, the bigger ones sat in the middle, and the biggest along the back. Father stood at the door and smoked, his face relaxed and smooth with content.

Then M. L'Estrange would begin. He would stand in front of us for a few minutes, his hands joined at his chest as if he were praying, his lean, lined face raised and immobile, and stare at us with those soft, sad eyes of his. Mesmerized, we stared back at him, our throats drying with anticipation, giggles stirring and promptly dying in our stomachs. Suddenly he would crack his fingers and say 'Would someone please open a window at the back of the auditorium?' or 'Would it be possible to have a spot-light switched on?' in a voice so unexpectedly quiet and persuasive that instinctively we all moved to do his bidding, so great was our relief that he had spoken, so hypnotic was his power over us. From then on he had us in the palm of his hand.

Although I saw his tricks every year for five or six years I remember only two of them. In one he knotted a heavy rope to a back tooth, gave the rope a tug, and out came a heavy wooden molar, the size of a turnip. The other trick I remember was with a rabbit who had dull, weary eyes like mother's. He sat the rabbit on father's table, surrounded it with four sheets of cardboard, covered it with a black cloth, and to our horror collapsed the box with a great thump of his fists. Of course the rabbit had disappeared. With a tired smile he produced it from under his jacket.

We knew that the show was over when M. L'Estrange walked over to where father stood, and led him by the hand to the middle of the classroom. Together they stood before us, both of them smiling and bowing (I was always embarrassed at father bowing, as if he had been part of the entertainment), while we clapped and cheered and whistled and stamped our feet. Then father made a speech of appreciation, thanked M. L'Estrange for 'including humble Beannafreaghan in his over-crowded itinerary,' reminded us to bring twopence each the next day—he paid the illusionist out of his own pocket, and during the following weeks badgered and cajoled his pupils to reimburse him—and gave us the rest of the afternoon off. It was then that I knew one of the few advantages of being the teacher's son: every year I was privileged to wheel M. L'Estrange's bicycle, with its precious box that held the rabbit and the giant tooth and the other sacred things securely sealed in a box attached to the carrier, from the school to our house. It was a quarter of a mile by road, and I was accompanied by a retinue of a dozen or more amateur illusionists who pantomimed around me, yanking out their teeth, and producing rabbits from schoolbags, and who offered me all the wealth of the pockets if I would allow them even to touch the rim of the mudguard.

M. L'Estrange's last visit to Beannafreaghan in the March of my tenth year is the one I remember most vividly because I had spent the whole doleful winter waiting for it. Father had decided that I was to be sent to a Jesuit boarding school in Dublin the following September (like so many of his grand plans this one fell through, too; when September came, mother got the Christian Brothers in the town to take me in as a day-pupil) and I had made up my mind that I would escape that terrible fate by getting M. L'Estrange, when he would come, to take me away with him as an apprentice illusionist. I knew that a busy man like him could do with an assistant who would organise his tours, and see to advance bookings, and look after his accoutrements. My plans were not altogether impracticable: I had a small bicycle of my own; and from my mentor I would learn his craft so that when he would retire I would become a professional illusionist myself. Throughout the year I had put all my pocket money into a cocoa tin so that when my apprenticeship would begin I would have a measure of financial independence. I told no one of my scheme. And that March, as I wheeled M. L'Estrange's bicycle from the school to the house, I remember watching the others clowning around me, and thinking how young and silly they were. Little did they know the wonderful future that was before me.

Father and M. L'Estrange sauntered in about half-an-hour later. As father's good humour unaccountably dwindled, the illusionist's increased. He bowed theatrically to mother, and addressed her as Madame, and I believe he would have raised her hand to his lips had she not pulled it away, and said in her flattest Tyrone accent,

'I suppose you're famished as usual, Mister, are you?'

'I'll not say no to a morsel, Madame,' said the illusionist with a roguish smile. 'I'll not say no.'

And for a man with such white hands and such a lean, patient face he had a huge appetite. Indeed so hungrily did he eat that father did all the talking, and M. L'Estrange only grunted 'I see' or 'Yes' or 'Imagine' between mouthfuls. When the meal was over father produced a bottle of whiskey, pulled two chairs up to the range, and the illusionist and himself sat talking and drinking at the fireside, as they did every year, until night came down on Beannafreaghan, and the whiskey was done.

That winter had been particularly severe. There was still snow on the hill-tops and the fields were rigid with black frost when M. L'Estrange came. We hadn't heard a bird in five months. Had I not had the evidence of the illusionist sitting in our kitchen and chatting to my father I would not have believed that spring was at hand. Their talk followed the usual pattern. At first they spoke of the satisfaction to be got from teaching school in a small rural community, 'striking a spark that could cause a conflagration,' as the illusionist called it, and from travelling around the countryside, 'opening the ready hearts of children to laughter,' as father called it. They agreed that each vocation had its unique rewards. Then they talked about the changes they had witnessed over the years: only really dedicated teachers now taught in decaying, shrinking schools; and only really altruistic troupers still entertained their pupils. Then they went away back to the past, and from there on it wasn't really a conversation at all, but two monologues spoken simultaneously, each man remembering and speaking his memories aloud. And eventually, when the bottle was empty, father became sarcastic.

Mother refused to be drawn into their talk. M. L'Estrange would try to engage her, but she shook him off quickly: 'You're nothing but a pair of bletherskites!'

Throughout the whole afternoon and evening she never stopped working, baking bread, washing clothes in the zinc bath, boiling nettles for the hens, scalding the milking tins, chopping vegetables for dinner the next day, all the time bustling about the kitchen so that she was constantly coming between me and the two men, and making so much noise with her buckets and basins that I missed a lot of what was being said. Not that I minded missing father's reminiscences—I had heard them so often that I knew them backways—but now that I was on the brink of a new life every word that M. L'Estrange had to say about his early career was of the utmost interest. But worse than the din she made, she tried to make conversation with me—'Have you no exercise to do?' 'Any fun at school today?' 'Why don't you go out for a run on your bicycle?' 'Are you not taking the dog out for a walk?'—and when I answered her in sharp monosyllables she invented jobs for me to do: feed the calf; bring in sticks; get water from the well; close the meadowgate. The result was that I heard only part of the monologues and witnessed only the last half of the row when M. L'Estrange called father a soured old failure and father called M. L'Estrange a down-at-heel fake and warned him never to set foot in Beannafreaghan again.

'The summer I qualified,' father was saying into his glass as I spread the sticks for the morning fire along the front of the range, 'I came first place in the whole of Ireland. And there wasn't a manager in the thirty-two counties who wouldn't have given his right arm for me. His right arm, Sir.'

'France is the country,' said M. L'Estrange, turning his rings idly. 'That's where they had appreciation. A hundred thousand francs for an hour's performance. La belle France.'

'Dublin—Cork—Galway—crying out for me. An old P.P. drove up the whole way from Kerry, three hundred and fifty miles, to ask me personally to take over a school in Killarney. "We would be honoured to have you, Mr. Boyle," he said.'

'Ah, the drawing-rooms of London in the early Twenties! Lords and ladies and all the quality of the land. Lloyd George once shook my hand and said it was a pleasure to see me perform.'

'But would I go? Oh, no! Beannafreaghan, I said. That's the place for me. Beannafreaghan. Because Beannafreaghan needed a teacher that had something more to give, just that little bit more than the other fellow.'

'A pleasure to see me perform. The year 1920. In Londonderry House, London, capital of the world.'

'I'm telling you, if I hadn't taken up the challenge that summer, bloody Beannafreaghan Primary School would have been closed down, and all the bloody children would have grown up illiterate.'

'Top of the bill in Leeds and Manchester and Glasgow and Brighton.'

'Bloody illiterates and too bloody good for them.'

'Mr. L'Estrange, Prince of the Occult.'

'Fifteen years ago the Very Reverend John Shiels, P.P., came out to me here, and stood in this very kitchen, and asked me—bloody-well begged me—to take over the new school in the town. Wasn't another man in the whole of County Tyrone competent to tackle it.'

'I drove my own car, and stayed in the best hotels, and picked and chose the engagements I wanted. There was respect for illusionists in those days, respect and admiration.'

'And what, said I straight out to him, and what would happen to Beannafreaghan?'

'I saw me ordering swank dinners for the whole cast and tipping the waiters with pound notes.'

'That never occurred to him. Oh, no! But it occurred to me. They may be country children, I said to him, and they may not have the most modern school building, but by God they deserve the best teacher in the country, top of my class the summer I qualified, and they're bloody-well going to have the best teacher in the country! I'm not going to desert them, I said to him.'

'My Lords, Ladies, and Gentlemen, things are not what they appear. The quickness of the hand deceives the eye. I was entrusted with the secret of this next act by the Sultan of Mysore—'

'And I didn't desert them. I'm bloody-well still here, amn't I? In spite of all the offers I got. Hundreds of them. Only fifteen years ago in this very kitchen—'

'In his white marble palace in the hills where the sun shines all day—'

'I'm still here! The proof of the pudding is in the eating!'

'It's all in the mind. The powers of the mind are beyond our comprehension.'

At that stage mother ordered me out to the byre with her to milk the cow. I held the hurricane lamp while she milked. She could do the job in five minutes when she wished, but that night she seemed to take hours at it. 'Hurry up! Hurry up!' I kept saying because I was afraid M. L'Estrange would have gone before we got back to the house.

'What do you want to be listening to the ravings of two drunk men for?' she said. 'I don't know what takes that trickster here anyway, upsetting everybody.' And she rested her forehead against the red cow's side and pulled the teats as if she never wanted the milking to end.

While we were out, the row began. In the still, frosty night we heard their angry voices as we turned the gable of the byre. Their talk always ended with father taunting the illusionist. But never until that night had M. L'Estrange answered him back; he just lifted his hat from behind the kitchen door and went off without a word into the darkness. But that year, when my whole future depended on him, he had to lose his temper.

'My God!' said mother. 'They'll kill each other.' And the pair of us ran up to the house.

M. L'Estrange was on the street, and father was standing in the doorway, and they were shouting at each other. Father held on to the doorposts for support, and the illusionist swayed back and forward and pointed an accusing finger at him. They were both ugly with hate.

'Go home to your hovel, wherever it is!' father roared. 'Bloody tramp!'

'Beannafreaghan is the place for you!' M. L'Estrange called back. 'The back end of nowhere!'

'And where did you pick up the name L'Estrange, eh? I know who you are, Monsieur Illusionist L'Estrange: your real name's Barney O'Reilly, and you were whelped and bred in a thatched cottage in County Galway!'

'They wouldn't give you a job in the town if there wasn't another teacher in the whole country!'

'You were never in London or Paris in your life! And your wee cheap tricks wouldn't fool a blind jennet!'

'You're stuck here till the day you die!'

'Mister Barney O'Reilly—fake!'

'A soured old failure!'

'Never put a foot in Beannafreaghan again or we'll set the dogs on you!'

'Don't you worry, Boyle. You'll never see me again.'

Mother sprang between them. She pushed father into the hallway and then wheeled on the illusionist.

'Get out of this place!' she spat at him with a fierceness I never saw in her before. 'Get away out of here and never darken the door again, you—you—you sham, you fake, you!'

Then she saw me standing with the hurricane lamp in my hand.

'Get inside at once!' she snapped. 'You should have been asleep hours ago.'

I did not dare disobey her, so mad was she. As I passed her on my way into the house she shoved me roughly in the back and bolted the door behind me.

Father was standing uncertainly in the middle of the kitchen floor. He tried to look defiantly at her.

'I told him a thing or two that he needed to—' he began.

'Get off to your bed,' said mother sharply. 'And shame on you making a scene like that before the child.'

'I told him a few home truths. I let him know what I thought of—'

'Shut up! Hasn't there been enough said for one night? Go and get some sleep, or you won't be fit to go to work tomorrow.'

As he lurched towards the door he tried to wink at me, but his two eyes closed.

'He forgot his beautiful hat!' he said, sniggering, lifting the shabby topper down from behind the door.

'Run after him with it,' said mother to me. 'I don't want him coming back to look for it. Run, child, run.'

That should have been my opportunity. Confused and frightened as I was with the shouting and the hate and the sickening sight of father and M. L'Estrange abusing each other, a part of my mind was still lucid, still urged me: Now, now, now. I saw the cocoa tin on the mantlepiece; I knew my bicycle, polished, oiled, pumped, was in the turf shed; I thought of the Dublin boarding school. But suddenly the dream that I had nursed all winter lost its urgency, required an effort and determination I couldn't muster. If by some miracle mother were to say, 'Go off with M. L'Estrange, son. Travel the world with him,' or if M. L'Estrange were to come back and say in his persuasive voice, 'Your son and I have planned to make a grand tour of Ireland and England and the whole of Europe,' then I would have floated off with him, and together we would have drifted happily from theatre to theatre, from country to country. But now I stood trembling, numbed, petrified with irresolution.

101

'Will you hurry up! He won't have got the length of the school yet,' said mother.

I unbolted the door and ran out into the hushed night.

I found M. L'Estrange on his hands and knees on the road below the byre. He was crawling towards his bicycle which lay spinning five yards beyond him. He smiled drunkenly up at me.

'It would appear, my friend, that my trusty steed and I parted company.'

The moonlight gave his face the pallor of a corpse. His long, thin fingers were spread out before him like the witch's in *Hansel and Gretel*.

'You forgot your hat.'

'Would you be kind enough to lift my bicycle for me? Once I get up on it nothing can stop me. The problem is—' He hiccoughed and mumbled, 'Excuse me'—'The problem is to get mounted, if you understand what I mean.'

I left the hat within his reach and went to lift the bicycle.

Before I got it I found the giant tooth lying on the road. Beside it was the square of black cloth. Further on I found four sheets of cardboard, and the mask, and a packet of balloons. I picked them up and carried them to the bicycle. It was then that I saw that the box on the carrier was open and empty. The rabbit! The rabbit had escaped! I was about to shout, to cry out to M. L'Estrange that his rabbit was gone when I saw it crouching beside the front wheel. Silently, cautiously I tiptoed over to it. But there was no need for silence or caution: it never moved. I gathered it gently in my arms and looked into its face. Its dull, weary eyes, mother's eyes, stared back at me, beyond me. Had its heart not tapped against my finger-tips I might have thought it was dead. I put it in the box on top of the black cloth and closed the lid.

M. L'Estrange was at my side.

'All set?' he said. 'Once more into the breach, dear friends, once more.'

He was wearing the top hat now, and it sat jauntily on the side of his head.

'As I say,' he went on, 'once I get mounted nothing can stop me, nothing in the wide world.' He put an arm on my shoulder to steady himself. 'As for you, my good friend, accept this little token from M. L'Estrange, Prince of the Occult.'

He slipped a coin into my hand. Then he gripped the handlebars, held the bicycle away from him, and said in his resonant voice that carried over the still, dead countryside, 'Au revoir!'

Then he moved off. He looked back at me to see was I watching him (I think he was going to attempt to get up on the bicycle). But when he saw me looking after him he waved to me and went on walking. A bend in the road hid him from me.

In the light of the kitchen I saw that he had given me a penny. I dropped it into the cocoa tin. Father was in bed, and mother was spooning my night porridge into a bowl.

'He's away, is he?' she asked.

I said he was.

'Sit down and take your supper,' she said. 'You're famished with the cold.'

'He gave me half-a-crown!' I blurted it out because I thought I was going to cry.

'Aye?' she said, giving me a shrewd look.

'And he said that he'll come to see me in the boarding school in Dublin.' I couldn't stop myself now. 'And he said that when I'm a big man he'll take me away with him and teach me all his magic and we'll see the seven seas and visit great palaces and carry red-and-gold parrots on our shoulders and drive about in big cars and stay in grand hotels and—and—and—'

Then the tears came, pouring out of me, and mother's

arms went round me, and I buried my face in her breast, and sobbed my heart out.

'And—and he was so drunk he fell off his bicycle and he could hardly walk. And only for me he would have lost his rabbit and his giant tooth and—'

'There, there, there,' said mother, rocking me against her and stroking the back of my head. 'It's all over now. It's all over. All over. It'll be forgotten in the morning. And before we know where we are, spring will be here, and you'll be away in Tracey's lorry to the bog to cut turf, and the birds will come back and begin nesting—'

'I told you a lie—it was a penny he gave me!'

'—and we'll bring the skep of bees up to the mountain for the heather,' she went on as if she hadn't heard me. 'And we'll whitewash the byre until it sparkles —remember the fun we had last year?—and before we know it will be summer, and we'll take the rug down to the meadow, and lie in the shade of the chestnut tree, and listen to the cow eating the clover, and we'll take a packet of biscuits with us and a can of buttermilk, and we'll have a competition to see who can drink it the quickest—remember last year?—and on the hottest day of summer—oh, it'll be so hot it will kill us to laugh!—we'll empty the well and climb down into it in our bare feet, and scrub it out, and yo-ho to each other down there—remember? remember?—and we'll laugh until we're weak, and oh my God, oh the great fun we'll have—oh dear God it'll be powerful—when the good weather comes.'

I stopped crying and smiled into her breast because every word she said was true. But it wasn't because I remembered that it was true that I believed her, but because she believed it herself, and because her certainty convinced me.

Ginger Hero

At the time I'm thinking about, the year Billy Brogan and I bought our own fighting-cock and matched him against the best birds in Ireland, you would never have suspected that Annie and Min were sisters. Ten years earlier, when Billy married Annie and I married Min, they were as like as two peas, although, strangely enough, it was Min who was the softer of the two then. But they had changed so much in the decade that you would have been hard put to find any resemblances between them. Annie had grown into a big, fat hearty woman who spent her days—except when she went to the cock-fights with Billy and me—in a wicker chair in front of the open hearth, her legs wide apart and an all-enveloping apron stretched across them, her chubby hands lying limp on her lap, and her gentle eyes waiting for half an excuse to stream with laughter. Maybe the house could have been tidier—there was nobody but Billy and herself to upset it, and Billy was as natty as an old maid—but she never seemed to notice it.

'Look at the state of the place!' she would say, struggling to her feet when you would go in. 'You would think I had a houseful of children!' And she would burst into such an infectious laugh that you forgot about the bucket of soiled clothes at the door and the breakfast dishes still on the table and the crumbs on the floor, and laughed with her. And although it was Billy who cleared a seat for you and wiped it clean with his hand it was Annie who made you feel at home.

Not that our house was much tidier. But then we had eight children and even if Min slaved from morning to night, as she did, there was always a toy somewhere to trip you or a row of steaming nappies to hide the fire from you. Poor Min, those first ten years were sore on her, made her thin and haggard and harrassed-looking. When I would see herself and Annie together I would wonder at how time had sharpened the one and mellowed the other: my wife with all the worries in the world and a wrinkle to show for every one, Billy's wife apparently without a care. I often thought that, if he had not had such an obsession about being childless, he could have been the happiest man in Donegal.

He was a strange buck, Billy. We were brothers-in-law; we worked together on Lord Downside's estate (Billy was land-steward, in charge of twenty of us); we spent most of our week-ends together; but for all that you never knew what he was thinking. He had been an amateur bantam-weight boxer in his single days and had never lost his pride in his physique. He was small and muscular and intense, without a superfluous ounce of flesh. His hair and eyebrows were sandy and his eyelashes so long that, when his eyes were closed, they touched the two tufts of bright ginger hair that sprouted from the top of his high cheek-bones. When you were talking to him he had the habit of tilting up that protruding chin of his, and closing his mouth in a sort of humourless grin, and hiding his eyes behind those silken lashes, and you could never tell whether he was listening to you or not. And yet, in spite of his remoteness and his quick temper and his passion for having everything correct, I always liked Billy.

The workmen of the estate admired him but they never warmed to him. They were jealous of the way he kept himself, of his careful appearance, of his measure of prosperity. They were all struggling on a meagre wage, just as I was myself, and although Billy could not have had more than a couple of pounds a week more than ourselves, he had only Annie and himself to support, and his paypacket was well able for that. The rest of us had armfuls of children to keep. In the early years of his marriage they would rag him about a family, and in the beginning he gave back as good as he got. But as time went on and there was still no sign of a child, they stopped joking to his face because he would go very still and his eyelashes would flicker. Behind his back, of course, they had many a good laugh about him: they wondered did The Bantam, as they called him, lead a married life at all; they wondered had his boxing career impaired him in some inexplicable way; they proposed all sorts of cures—from putting him on a diet of goat's milk to calling on Annie themselves. Then, when they made ribald jokes about Annie, I would tell them to shut up, not because she was my sister-in-law, but from a sense of loyalty to Billy; maybe, too, because she reminded me so much of the Min I had married.

There was a row in our house every Sunday Billy and I went to a cock-fight.

'Traipsing about like tinkers, and gambling behind wee hills, and mixing with all the good-for-nothings in the country, and running from the police!' Min would snap at me. 'It's all very well for Billy Brogan that has neither chick nor child. But you—you have responsibilities, if you only knew it!' And when Annie began travelling around in the van with us she went mad altogether. 'Oh, aye! Go ahead and enjoy yourselves! Leave me here to wrestle with your children! Go ahead and have your fun! Since the day I married you what have I ever been but a house-keeper and a nurse-maid! Go on! Go on! Gamble your few shillings away!'

These tirades were for my ears alone. When Billy would call for me she would be as sweet as could be. 'So you're off for a bit of fun, Billy? Well, why wouldn't you? It's going to be a nice afternoon. Take care of yourselves now, and good luck!' Whatever it was about him she had a powerful respect for him. I often thought, watching her looking at him in his neat Sunday suit and his immaculate shirt and his shining shoes, that she was not at all sure her sister had not got the better man. And out in the van, with Annie wedged between him and me, and seeing her look up so honestly into the fair, uncommunicative face of his, I knew that she had no doubts at all.

Billy was an expert on cocks. I had never seen a fight until he brought me to one, three or four years after we had married; and although he had become interested in the sport only a year before I did he had made a study of every detail of it, just as he had studied crop rotation and pig-breeding and Ayrshire cows. So when Spittles Sheridan sent word to me that he had a promising year-old bird for sale I could not wait to tell Billy.

'All he wants is £10,' I said. 'It's for nothing, man! A gift! You know yourself that his birds have the best of stuff in them.'

His mouth was shut tight and his eyelashes slept on his cheeks.

'Look, Billy,' I went on, 'this is our chance. We'll never make money betting on strange birds. But with a bird of our own, trained by us, we could make a wee fortune. £5 each is all that it will cost us. We'll make that much—three times that—on the first time it's out. What do you say?'

'I'll think about it,' he said, without opening his eyes.

'Think be damned! There's no time to think about it. If we don't take it before the week-end Tony McGrenra or Hoppy Reilly or McHugh from Frosses will have grabbed it.'

'Colour?'

'Ginger. And Spittles claims—'

'Age?'

'Twelve months.'

'You're sure he has never set it?'

'He swears he hasn't.'

'Weight?'

'For God's sake, man, I haven't seen the thing myself yet!'

He opened his eyes then and smiled slowly at me.

'You're interested or you're not—which is it?' I said sharply, because his calmness always angered me when I was enthusiastic.

'I'll tell you what, Tom,' he said. 'We'll go and have a look at it on Saturday. Satisfied?'

I was not satisfied but I knew I would wait.

'I hope we're not too late then, that's all.'

'We won't be,' he said. 'Don't let that worry you. We won't be.'

He was right, of course: the bird was still there. I was disappointed in it. I thought its legs should have been longer and I did not like the easy way it carried itself. I expected a mature cock, with fiery eyes and jerky steps and lightning movements of the head and neck, but this bird was thin and undeveloped and domesticated.

Spittles stood behind us.

'It's nothing but a broody hen, that,' I whispered to Billy who was crouched on the floor of the byre. 'Come on away home.'

He held it in his hands—it sat there, patient, docile—and under the ginger feathers and over the white transparent flesh his gentle fingers explored the breast and the back and the long neck, kneading, pressing, massaging, caressing slowly and with assurance, until the bird's eyes became drunken and its head rose and fell like an old man dozing before a fire.

'It's a bloody chicken,' I said into his ear. 'It couldn't beat its way out of a wet paper bag! It wouldn't last five seconds against a good crow!'

He did not hear me. The bird was sotted now and spread its toes in an ecstasy of pleasure. But still he worked at it, rubbing its thighs between fingers and thumb.

'Billy!' I hissed. 'That thing will never be a cock!'

'What?' he said, aware of me for the first time.

'Are you coming home?'

He put the bird carefully on the ground, watched it stagger, shake itself, and walk away; then he got to his feet. Spittles came between us, his chin wet as usual with saliva.

'Yes, boys? A great bird, eh? One hell of a fine bird, eh?'

'He'll make a good mattress,' I said. 'After some sparrow kills him with one peck.'

'Ah, now Tom—'

'£7,' said Billy.

'For God's sake, Billy!' I said.

'£7?' Spittles began to slobber. 'Ah, now, boys, boys, boys—'

'£7,' Billy repeated.

'Are you out of your mind?' I said.

Billy ignored the two of us and watched the bird dab at an old shoe.

'McHugh will give me £10 if I ask him,' said Spittles. 'All I have to do is give the word.'

'£7. Take it or leave it,' said Billy quietly.

'Wait a minute, Billy—' I began.

'Settled!' said Spittles. 'The bird's yours. Give me the money now.'

Billy paid him in single notes. Then he put the cock under his jacket and we left.

'What the hell do you mean by buying a chicken like that!' I said when we were out of earshot. 'You might at least have asked me for my advice. £7 down the drain—that's what that is!'

He stopped at the door of the van and raised his long chin at me.

'You don't have to go halves in this if you don't want to, Tom.'

'It's not the money. £3/10/0 is neither here nor there,' I lied in boast, as I often did with Billy. 'It's just that you might have asked my advice before you took the damned thing.'

'Make up your mind, Tom. You want to go halves or you don't.'

'It's just that I think we could have got a better—'

'Which is it?'

'Here's your money,' I said, thrusting my share into his hand. 'I only hope you know what you're doing.'

'I do,' he said, blinking his lashes at me.

When I told Min of the deal, she scolded and sulked and scolded again; and I found myself adopting Billy's tactics with me—I behaved as if I did not hear her. That set her crazy altogether.

'You'll be away every week-end now!' she accused. 'Have you no thought at all for your family? What sort of a husband and father are you?'

I did not answer.

'Don't you know the neighbours are all laughing at you behind your back?' she went on. 'Hanging on to Billy and Annie as if you had no home of your own! Haven't I borne your children for you? Isn't the house clean? Don't I cook your food and mend your clothes and wear myself out looking after you? Is that not enough for you?'

But I had not Billy's control, and I shouted back at her, and for days on end we were at one another's throat. To keep out of her way I spent more and more time at Billy's house after I finished work on the estate.

It was Annie who christened the bird Ginger Hero and it was she who cooked its corn-meal and chopped its hard-boiled eggs and minced its raw meat and rubbed it down each day with ammonia and alcohol. Billy looked after its training and trimmed its hackle- and rump-feathers. I had no part in its rearing. Indeed, if I as much as mentioned the bird in the house, Min lit on me. 'Oh, surely, surely! Mister Thomas, the sporting gentleman with eight children! He's only a labourer on the estate but he owns a fighting-cock, if you don't mind! And what matter if his children can afford butcher's meat only on a Sunday as long as his wee birdie can have the best of fillet steak seven days a week—Fridays and all! What respect can a man like that have for the laws of God when he puts a brute bird before his own family!'

But when the cock began to make a bit of money for us, at Ballybofey and Letterkenny and Strabane, she quit nagging at me and would even bring herself to ask, 'I suppose you'll be travelling somewhere next week-end, will you?' She was not greedy, Min, but she had a powerful regard for money—I suppose because we never had any.

There was no denying that Billy knew how to handle a bird. Six months after we bought that cock from Spittles its own mother would not have recognised it. It was never big and it never weighed a gram over three pounds seven ounces, but it developed great shoulders and a deep chest and a neck of iron, and when you set it in the pit you could see the trembles of the muscles in its legs and feet. But it was none of those things, nor its leather skin, nor its stamina, nor its courage, nor its tenacity, that made it the champion cock of Ireland, but its eyes, its pale calm eyes which revealed nothing, neither anger, nor fear, nor anxiety, nor pain, and which could judge to a fraction of a second when to attack and when to retreat, when to strike and when to withhold, when to swing down those deadly spurs on a stationary head, when to go for the kill.

'The eyes are the best part of him, Billy,' I would say. 'Man, with eyes like that, he could tackle a hawk!'

'Maybe, Tom. Maybe,' Billy would say in his calm way.

'I'm not taking away from the work you did on him, mind you. But you'll admit he started off to a great advantage with eyes like that. Didn't he now?'

And Billy would smile with pleasure, and the ginger tufts on his cheek bones would rise and touch the ends of his sandy lashes.

But although Billy spent one hour every day working with it, and although I had the job of cutting its comb

112

before a main, it was to Annie it would run when the three of us would go out to the pen at the back of the house, and she would sweep it up into her arms, and it would rub its head against her face, and she would coo and whisper into its ear, and it would let itself be pressed against her big breasts, and she would fondle and caress it as if neither Billy nor I were present. I never could tell whether she loved that cock for its own sake, or whether she loved it because it was Billy's; but love it she did, that was clear; and there was no doubt that it was fond of her. But the strange thing about that bird was that it shrank from her every so often, on those days when we had a fight for it. We would go out to the pen as usual, and Annie would hold out her arms to it and call to it, 'Ginger! Ginger Hero! Come, boy! Come, come, come!' But it knew, by some strange instinct, that this was a day for the pit, and it would shy away from her and go cautiously to Billy, its head erect, its legs lifting stiffly. She would laugh then, laugh until her whole fat body shook. And she would wag her finger at it and shout raucously, 'You're a bold wee rascal! That's what you are! A naughty wee rogue!' But for all her laughing, you could see that she was hurt. And I would wonder, looking at that wary-eyed bird, at the two birds he was and not one at all: Annie's during the week to spoil and pet; and on the morning of a main Billy's bird only, because Billy was the only one of us it would allow to put on its spurs, and Billy alone could set it in the pit—it would have pecked the hands off Annie or me.

It fought eight fights in a row and never lost a feather. It blinded Hoppy Reilly's wee blackie outside Castlederg and killed McHugh's brown cock in five minutes flat at the main at McHugh's own home-ground of Frosses. They brought cocks up from Clonmel and they brought cocks down from Inishowen and it scattered them all. Of course, Billy was very careful of it. They tried to get him to pitch the Ginger Hero against two-year-olds and against birds of four pounds and over. Then they tried to persuade him to take part in a Welsh main—a day's contest with eight cocks, the four victors then being paired, then the two—but Billy was having none of that: he knew that they knew that nothing ruins a fighting-cock quicker than hacking him like that. (If the bird had been mine I would have agreed because the odds would have been good; and as Ginger won fight after fight, and as his reputation spread, the best we could get was even money.) When everything else failed some of them even reported us to the police. But Spittles Sheridan tipped us off, and the night the police called at Billy's house there was not the trace of a cock to be seen: Annie had it under the blankets with her!

The good times lasted a year. We travelled down to Galway and Mayo, and over to Cavan and Meath, and once—for the sake of a side bet of £30—down to Kilkenny to meet a famous white cock that was said to have been reared on raw mackerel and gin. Maybe it was, too. But the day we fought him he must have been in the D.Ts.

Annie enjoyed the outings as much as any of us. She sat between Billy and me, and laughed, and joked, and waved out to strangers on the roadside, and put her arm round Billy, and rested her head on his shoulder, and sang ballads in her easy voice, and chatted as heedlessly as a school-girl. Many a time I found myself watching them in the driver's mirror: Annie's face so relaxed with happiness, Billy's quiet, calm, secretive. And then I would think of Min and myself, and remember our courting days, and wonder with fresh surprise at the way our lives had wilted so rapidly into an endless, ungenerous squabble. And I would be seized by a quick desire to grab Billy and shake him and shout into his ear, 'What sort of a stupid bastard are you? What more do you want? Look at her, man! Look at her!' But I never grabbed him or shook him or shouted at him; and my thoughts invariably shifted from him to her; and many a time I found myself wondering had Min really

114

been the softer of the two in their single days, or had I only imagined that she had been.

That was on the way *to* a fight, when our senses were keen, when we were all three of us alert with anticipation, when the bird could not be touched by anyone but Billy. But on the way home we were always fatigued, and talked little, and the cock was all Annie's again, and she held it in her arms, and stroked it until it fell asleep. Sometimes Annie herself slept, and Billy and I would be left staring at the white columns of the headlights.

'You wouldn't think of selling it?' I asked him the night we drove up from Kilkenny.

Winter was beginning, and the van was cold, and he had taken off his jacket and put it round Annie while she slept.

'Billy!'

'What's that?'

'You wouldn't think of selling, would you?'

I had a vision of me handing over my share to Min and of her stuck for once for something to say.

He shook his head from side to side.

'He's at his prime, I'll grant you,' I said. 'But from now on he won't be getting better.'

'I'm not selling yet,' he said.

'What are you waiting for? Until he's stiff? Until he's lamed or blinded?'

'No, Tom.'

'What then?'

He took his eyes off the road and looked at me over Annie's sleeping figure.

'I'm going to match him against Captain Robson's Tawny Tiger.'

'You're what!'

'It's all arranged. Next Saturday fortnight, at Grasslough, in County Monaghan.'

'Billy, are you mad? That's not a cock—that's an ostrich! He's a ton weight! There's not a bird in the country would face up to him!'

115

'It's the only challenge there's left, Tom. Anyhow, there's no point in discussing it. The match is settled.'

'When was it settled? Who settled it? Was I consulted, was I?'

He ignored me.

'I'm going to prove that my bird is as good as the best in the country.'

'*Your* bird!'

He did not even look in my direction.

'I'm going to show them,' he said, almost in a whisper. 'Just you wait and see. I'm going to show them.'

Despite my doubts, or because Billy was never wrong, I decided to put all the savings I had on the Grasslough fight. I asked Min to give me back the rent and house-keeping money for that week. But she refused.

'Gamble the shirt off your back for all I care!' she jeered. 'But the children at least are going to have a roof over their heads and a bite in their mouths.'

Every time we fought now she flung the children at me.

'Look, Min,' I said, 'you'll get your money back. I only want to be able to put on a decent bet.'

'A *decent* bet! That's a good one!'

'All right! Keep it!' I roared.

'I will, Mister Thomas,' she spat back. 'Don't you worry, I will!'

I believe I was angry enough to strike her then. But the children were playing outside the kitchen window. I pulled my coat down from the wall and went across the fields to Billy's house.

Billy was putting the cock into the back of the van and Annie was holding the door open for him. I called and waved to them, and she turned and smiled and waved back to me. She must have had herself harnessed up in all sorts of unaccustomed corsets because I remember noticing how slender and youthful she looked; with her soft smooth face and her laughing eyes she looked as beautiful as Min had looked the morning I married her. Before I reached them she went into the house.

'All set?' I said to Billy.

'Look, Tom,' he said, glancing quickly after her. 'Will you do me a favour?'

'Surely, Bill.'

'About this fight—and Annie. She thinks it's just an ordinary main. She doesn't know the Tawny Tiger's record. Don't tell her, will you?'

'She must know! She has heard all the talk about him, hasn't she?'

'I'm telling you. She doesn't realise how good he is. If she did she wouldn't want the Hero to be matched against him.'

'But when she sees—'

'You won't tell her, will you?

Annie came out of the house.

'How long will it take us to get there?' she asked.

'A couple of hours,' said Billy. 'In we get and off we go.'

'I was just looking at you when I was coming up the hill, Annie,' I said. 'It's younger you're getting.'

She gave a peal of laughter.

'Listen to him!' she said, throwing her arms around Billy. 'Why don't you say nice things like that to me?'

He waited until she released him.

'We'll be there before noon,' he said. 'Off we go.'

We climbed into the van and drove off, and Annie never stopped singing until we arrived at Grasslough two hours later.

As soon as I saw Captain Robson my first thought was: Min, if only you were here! Because he was an even finer looking man than Lord Downside, and she thought Downside was the finest gentleman in the world. He was English, well over six feet, straight as a rush, and dressed in an elegant dark suit and a canary waistcoat. He invited us into his house for drinks, and discussed the fight—he called it 'the duel'—as briskly as if he were

117

planning a day's harvesting; no winking, no nudging, no mumbling behind the backs of hands, no nervousness of a police raid, no sly questions about age or weight or diet. We had never seen anything like this before. Annie looked about her with big wondrous eyes. Even the cool Billy was impressed. I let him do all the talking.

Then the Captain brought us out to a huge hay-shed and showed us his pit.

'It is regulation,' he said. 'Usual eighteen feet in diameter. Surround sixteen inches high. Sawdust floor. Satisfactory?'

'Grand,' said Billy.

'Good. Now we'll have a look at Tawny Tiger.'

He cracked his fingers, and a workman who had been standing at a distance came running up.

'Fetch the Tiger, O'Boyle,' he said, and O'Boyle scuttled off.

'I've been thinking about this duel,' he went on. 'And I've come to the conclusion that it isn't fair to ask you to risk your bird against a heavier and more experienced cock.'

'We're agreeable to—' Billy began.

'No, it is not fair. So in the circumstances, since this is more a contest for prestige, I have made two decisions: there will be no gambling on this duel; but if your bird wins, I will give you £200; and if I win, I will be amply rewarded by knowing that I own the best cock in Ireland. Satisfactory?'

'Suits me,' said Billy.

'And your friend?' said the Captain.

'Suits me,' I said, because that was what Billy had said.

'Good. O'Boyle will be judge. I can vouch for his integrity. Let's get started, shall we?'

Annie stood between Billy and me at the edge of the pit. She had not opened her mouth since we had arrived at Robson's place. Now she murmered something to Billy, but he did not answer her. He had our cock under his jacket and he was stroking it slowly and deliberately as if he were conveying last minute instructions to it. She turned to me.

'Tom—' She spoke in a whisper.

'What is it?'

'I-I-I have a queer feeling about this place.'

'It will be all over in no time,' I said.

'It's the Hero I'm thinking about. Will he be hurt, Tom?'

I pretended to laugh.

'Hurt? He won't even be tickled!'

'Could we call it off, Tom? Is it too late to call it off?'

'Easy, Annie. Easy. There's nothing to worry about.'

She did not hear what I said. Her lips were parted, and her breath was coming in shallow gasps, and her eyes roamed anxiously around that great shed as if she were taking a mental note of the exits.

My heart sank when I saw the size of Tawny Tiger, and when Ginger Hero was set in the pit the Captain's bird seemed to grow even bigger. It was no consolation that at last Billy had made a mistake. I would willingly have surrendered the money that was sweating in my pocket if I could have grabbed our bird and run out of that eerie shed that echoed and re-echoed in its high roof with every tiny sound that was made under it. Not that there was much noise; only a few clipped words from the Captain, and the starting order from O'Boyle—'Let the cocks fight'. Until that moment I never knew how much I loved the familiar hissing and booing and cheering and squabbling and the vulgar comments and the swearing. This orderly, superior set-up was no sport. It was unnatural.

The Tiger barged into battle, wings wide, neck arched, eyes burning, body high and poised. Ginger Hero crouched, waiting, his eyes dead, watchful, wary. For a second they were three feet apart; then, simultaneously, they attacked. There was the dull thud of their bodies, the click of spur against spur, and the Hero was

119

bowled over. At first I could see nothing but the broad back of the Tiger, and its plunging head, and its stabbing feet. I thought: My God, it has punctured the Hero's throat! But then I saw our cock's legs working like pistons, scratching, scratching at the Tiger's breast; the spurs were not sticking, could not penetrate the feathers and skin; but although the Tiger was mauling his head and neck, those never stopped working until the left spur penetrated, and the Tiger was flung from his dominance.

I looked at Annie. Her hands were pressed to the sides of her head. I glanced beyond her to Billy. He might have been asleep, so calm he looked. Then I saw his lips moving, and heard him breathe. 'Yes. Yes. Yes. Yes. Yes. Yes. . . ,' without ceasing, almost inaudibly, as if he were praying devoutly.

The first blood was drawn. It flowed from below the Hero's right eye. But before I could take a closer look they were battling again.

The Tiger made his second charge, but this time our bird kept his feet. Then they both went down, spurs locked, necks linked, two balls of feathers rolling over and over. The Hero freed himself first, caught the Tiger's head still for an unguarded second, and spiked it with such force that, for the moment those tiny needles gored into the Tiger, our bird was levered two feet into the air.

It was then that the Tawny Tiger went mad, so mad that he turned his back on our cock, and went tearing around the circumference of the pit, with his great blazing head straining to the roof, and his wings trailing through the saw-dust, and his beak open and emitting a throaty, hissing sound. He was so mad that he did not know where he was or what it was he was supposed to be doing. Then, suddenly, he remembered. He stopped at the head of the pit, surveyed the ring, spotted the Hero, and with a cry that was almost human in its abandon, half-flew, half-raced at our cock. They met in the centre of the pit, and there—without once separating again—they spiked and speared and stabbed and savaged one another with all the concentrated fury that was in them.

I did not watch all of it. For the first time in my life I felt sickened by it. There, in the silence of that shed, with no sound but the odd quick squawk of sudden pain and the sibilant 'Yes. Yes. Yes. Yes' of Billy, with no cheering, no laughing, no fun, no ribaldry, that savage, deadly battle for life was too tense, too heartless. Sometimes I closed my eyes. Sometimes I looked at Annie. Her hands never left her head; her body was as motionless as a statue. Sometimes I watched the Captain's pale, evil face—for now it was evil. Sometimes I looked at O'Boyle. But always my gaze went back to the cocks. They were spent now. Only their endless courage kept them going, kept them plunging at each other.

The Tawny Tiger was on his side. The brownish-yellow feathers of his body were wet and splashed with saw-dust, and his neck, almost naked, glistened like raw meat. His legs were stiff and quivering.

Over him stood our tattered cock. He balanced on his left foot, and with his right he spiked the head of his opponent with slow, drunken, involuntary movements. He was scarcely able to stand, but he kept on spiking as if that were the only movement he was capable of.

Annie's scream shattered the muted silence of that shed. Her hands went up to her hair; she flung her head back; her mouth opened; and a wild, animal cry broke from her lips. It was a wail of terrible agony.

'Stop it!' she moaned. 'Stop it! Stop it! Stop it!'

I gripped her arm.

'Annie! Annie!'

She shook me off and fell on Billy, pounding his shoulders with her fists.

'Stop it!' she screamed. 'Stop it! Stop it! Stop it! Stop it!'

121

He did not feel the first blows, so engrossed was he in the fight. Then, his eyes darted to her for a second—'Take her away, for Christ's sake!' he muttered to me—and went back to the ring again.

I tried to hold her arms but she had the strength of three women. She clawed at his neck and shoulders and tried to push him into the pit.

'Take her away! She'll ruin everything!' he snapped. 'Take her away!'

'Stop it, Billy! Oh, God, stop it, Billy ! Please, Billy. Please!'

He swung on her then, his face stretched with fury, put his two hands against her body, and flung her violently back from him. She fell on the floor behind him. He wheeled back to watch the end of the fight. She lay there, sobbing.

I lifted her gently off the ground and led her, trembling, out of the shed. We passed the Captain and O'Boyle. They did not see us although we came between them and the pit.

Since we had married I had never seen Min cry. When she should have cried she had jeered or sulked. And now, with Annie, I was awkward and fumbling. I took her to the back of the van, and climbed in beside her, and spoke to her as I had not spoken since my courting days. Her teeth were chattering and she clung to me. I held her to me, and whispered to her, and covered her face with gentle kisses, and stroked her smooth, soft face with my rough hands. The sobbing stopped. And then, fiercely, wildly, she pulled me to her, and kissed me again and again. And in the moment before the singing blood drowned my thinking I imagined I heard her say, 'Billy, Billy, Billy. . . .'

We were sitting in the front when Billy joined us. The cock lay on its side on the upturned palms of his hands. Its feet were still stabbing the empty air.

'It's all over! He won! He won!' Billy was breathless with triumph. 'Quick! Where's the brandy?'

122

'It's in the back, Billy,' I said.

He held the cock out to Annie.

'There, Annie. He's yours now.'

'No,' she said coldly, turning her face away. 'No, no, no. Not today.'

He looked quickly at her and then at me. His cheekbones went up and his eyes went wary. You never could tell what Billy was thinking.

'Give the cock to me,' I said quickly, because his steady eyes were probing me and I was embarrassed.

I took the bird from him and pretended to examine its wounds. Billy still stood looking in at us.

'I'll be back shortly,' he said at length. 'The Captain is counting out the prize money.'

I climbed into the back and washed the bird in alcohol. Its eyes were glazed and its heart-beat irregular. I knew it would be dead before we got home, but I did all the jobs to it as tenderly as Annie would have done them.

'Will you tell Billy?' I said to her.

She sat staring straight in front of her.

'It doesn't matter,' she said.

'I believe he suspects,' I said.

'It doesn't matter, Tom,' she said. 'It doesn't matter at all.'

Then Billy came back and tossed a roll of notes on to my knees.

'How is he?' he asked.

'Fair. Only fair.'

He looked at Annie.

'I'm—I'm sorry I lost my temper back there.'

She snorted through her nose.

'Let's get home,' she said irritably. 'It's a long journey.'

His eyelashes fluttered. He smiled uncertainly.

'Home it is,' he said. 'Home it is.' And he started up the engine.

On our way through the town of Omagh I heard the sound of the cock's feet scraping the side of the van, and

I knew it was his dying kick. But I said nothing to the others, because none of us had spoken since the journey had begun, and because I knew they must have heard the sound too.

Three weeks later Billy got a job as land-steward on an estate in the south of England, and Annie and himself left Donegal for good. Min sent them a card that first . Christmas but they did not reply. We never heard from them again. The parish priest told me, one Sunday after Mass, that he had had a letter from Annie, asking for a copy of her marriage certificate.

'Must be a christening in the family,' he said. 'Takes the English air!' And he smiled roguishly. I did not tell Min.

With my share of the winnings of the Grasslough fight she had opened a small shop in the shed beside the house. She sold ice-cream and groceries and sweets to the families who lived on the estate. There was little profit in it—on a good week she made £2 clear, and she would boast, 'Between us we're making as much as the land-steward now!'—but getting away from the kitchen and the children, and meeting the neighbours, and chatting to them made a new woman of her. She put on weight, and her face lost some of its creases. And every night, when I got home from work, she sat opposite me on the other side of the fire, and told me all the gossip of the countryside. She was always a good mimic, Min, and many a night she had me in stitches laughing at her.

She tried to persuade me to take up cock-fighting again; 'A man needs a hobby,' she said. But I had enough of cocks.

'I tell you what, then, Tom,' she said, her face lighting up. 'We'll call this shop after that bird of yours—what's this his name was?—Ginger Love?—Ginger Hope?'

'Ginger Hero,' I said.

'That's it!' she laughed girlishly. 'We'll call the shop The Ginger Hero—so that we'll never forget that it was him that turned our luck!'

'Right, Min,' I said. 'The Ginger Hero it will be.'

And the next day—it was a Saturday—I bought a tin of black paint and a length of timber and printed the three words as steadily and as evenly as I was able.

Among the Ruins

There was no doubt about it, Joe thought as he sat in the car and waited for his wife and children to join him: Margo was simply wonderful. She had had an early lunch for them; she had so cleverly primed the children —who usually detested these organized outings with their parents—that they were still curious about the destination, and eager to be off. The whole idea of going back to Corradinna had been hers, and although it was early summer and the weather would probably have been good anyhow, she had managed to choose the best Sunday of the year so far. Yes, Margo was simply wonderful.

When she had first mentioned her plan to him the previous Friday night, he felt unaccountably stubborn. 'Corradinna? What the hell would take us there? There's nothing there now but the ruins of the old place.'

'You still must have some curiosity about it,' she had urged. 'Even if it's only to see if you have lost the feel of the place.'

'Feel?' he had said, deliberately misunderstanding her. 'You know me—I'm not sentimental that way.'

'And for the children's sake, too. I would like them to see where you lived when you were their age. It would be good for them.'

'I don't see the point,' he had said. 'I don't see the point at all.'

But she had persisted, and that night and the next day his stubbornness gave way to a stirring of memory and

126

then to a surprising excitement that revealed itself in his silence and his foolish grin. And now that they were about to set off, there was added a great surge of gratitude to her for tapping this forgotten source of joy in him. She knew and understood him so well.

Mary and Peter sat impatiently on the edge of the back seat. She was her mother in miniature.

'Now, Mammy! Where? Where?' she begged. 'You promised you would tell us now.'

Margo turned to watch their faces. 'We are going to Donegal—'

'I want to go to the beach,' Peter broke in.

'—to see where your daddy used to live and play when he was your age.'

'Are we, Daddy? Really?' Mary asked.

'Looks like it,' said Joe, smiling helplessly.

'I still want to go to the beach,' said Peter doggedly.

Mary caught his arm. 'Can't you hear, stupid? We're goint to see where Daddy used to play when he was a little boy.'

'Where's that?' Peter asked cautiously.

'Away, away far off in Donegal,' said Margo. 'And if you're going to behave like that, you are going to spoil the day on all of us.'

'So stop whining, boy!' said Mary severely, imitating her mother with unconscious accuracy.

'I'm not whining.'

'You were a minute ago.'

'That'll do, the both of you! Do you want to ruin the day on your daddy?'

'What's the name of the place?' Mark asked.

'Corradinna,' said Joe.

'Corradinna,' said Peter, sampling the word. 'That's a funny name.' He turned to his sister, screwed up his face and said in a man's voice, 'Corradinna'.

'Corradinna,' she piped back at him.

They fell into a fit of laughing at their private joke.

After the first hour, they became restless. They changed sides—Mary behind Margo and Peter behind Joe. Later they changed back again. Then they quarrelled over the exact position of the imaginary line down the middle of the back seat. Then Peter wanted the windows down and Mary wanted them up; she was cold, she said. Then Margo asked Joe to pull in to the side, because Peter had to go out for a minute. Then, five miles farther on, Mary had to get out. It was the usual pattern for a Sunday afternoon outing, but today it did not irk Joe, because Margo had assumed complete control, soothing, compromising, reprimanding, keeping peace, and the children's bickering claimed only a fraction of his attention. She was allowing him the uninterrupted luxury of remembering, hearing sounds and voices and cries he thought he had forgotten.

Corradinna lay at the foot of Errigal mountain, a pyramid of granite that rose three thousand feet out of the black bog earth. Because it marked the end of their journey and was visible for the last twenty miles, Joe found himself leaning over the driving wheel, as if to see beyond the folds of hills that still lay before him.

'Easy,' said Margo. 'You're going too fast.'

'Am I?'

'You'll be there time enough. Do you want the children to get sick?'

At this moment, I don't give a damn, he thought without callousness; at this moment, with Meenalaragan and Pigeon Top on my left and Glenmakennif and Altanure on my right. Because these are my hills, and I knew them before I knew wife or children.

'Joe! Do you hear me?'

'Sorry,' he said, slowing down. 'Sorry.'

Every Saturday morning, with the two Lakeland terriers, just for a walk. You got to the top of one hill and stood there with your arms opened out to the wind and watched the dogs, crazed with the scent of a fox, scramble down before you, and you ran down after them and then up the next incline and down the next and up and down and up and down, and when you got home in time for dinner, the dogs were so fatigued that they could not sleep but lay restlessly on the cold flags of the kitchen floor, staining the stone under their noses with circles of damp. It is all coming back to me, he thought.

They left the car at the side of the road and walked up the grass-covered track to the ruins of the house. The roof had fallen in, and the windows were holes in the walls. Someone had carved his initials on the doorpost: 'J.M. . . . NOV. 1941.' Mary, convinced that there must still be something spectacular to be seen after so long a journey, began asking petulantly, 'Show us now, Mammy! Show us now!'

'This is it all,' Margo said. 'This is where your daddy used to play.'

'Who did he play with? What games did he play?'

'He used to play around the house here. And around those fields. Why don't you and Peter go exploring for yourselves, while your daddy and I look around here?'

'I have seen everything,' said Peter.

'You couldn't have,' said Margo. 'Go on, off with the pair of you! Your daddy and I will be around here somewhere. And if you get tired walking, go and sit in the car.'

When they had gone, she said to Joe, 'Was that the garden?'

'Yes,' he said, and walked away from her. She followed him.

The garden, the path, the gooseberry tree. And the chestnut. That is our swing. Our father ties the ropes across that branch, and we soar up and out over the laneway. And Mother cries, 'Careful, Joe! Careful!' and Susan, my sister, squeals, 'Higher! Higher!' and Father comes round the side of the house and says, 'Is the cow not in yet, boy?' and Susan says, 'I'll get it, Joe's busy swinging'. Off she runs like a fairy thing, and because she is gone, the boy who is I jumps down and runs after her, and when he catches up with her, they dawdle along the bank of the river—river? What river? This trickle of water? Where did the river go?—and he says, 'Dare you to jump the river.' 'How much?' 'Half the hazelnuts under my bed.' 'It's a bet.' And she grips her lips between her teeth and takes a wild, gangling leap and lands in the middle of the water. They laugh and take off her shoes and wring out her socks and, the wetting suddenly forgotten, stroll across the fields to the wood—but where is the wood? It couldn't be this sad little cluster of oaks!—until they come to the bluebell patch. 'We'll bring home bluebells to Mother.' Susan's arms are out. 'Fill them,' she says. 'No. These will do.' 'Fill them. Fill them.' 'We forgot the cow.' 'The cow! Quick. The cow!' Another race across the meadow, through the gap in the hedge, clean over the river this time, because there is no bet to tighten your legs. And home, home, back past the barn. The barn, with its treasures—parts of bicycles, bits of beehives, a tea chest of old clothes, the drumsticks. Susan sings, and he accompanies her with the drumsticks on a cigar box. She dresses up in a long, tan-coloured silk frock, strap-over shoes, a hugh picture hat—all her mother's. She sings 'Red sails in the sunset,' over and over again, because the first line is the only one she knows.

'Susan! Joe! Teatime!'

Hide! Hide! Down to the bower at the foot of the garden! Oh, the laughing in that bower! Laughing till they are sore. And then, as soon as they sober up, one of them pulls a face, and they are off again. Oh, God, the pain of that laughing! 'What do you two laugh at?' Father says. 'You would think to look at you that you were a pair of half-wits. What *do* you laugh at, anyhow?' And that makes them worse, because Susan twitches her eyes or shrugs her shoulders, and if they were to be killed they couldn't stop now at all.

'Joe?' Margo's voice at his elbow. 'What are you smiling at, Joe?'

Suddenly he was alert, wary. 'Remembering,' he said.

'Remembering what?'

'The bower. Susan and myself in the bower.'

'What was it?'

'A place . . . a sort of hideout at the foot of the garden there. It's gone now. I looked.'

'What did you do there?'

'Laugh. Laugh, mostly.'

Clouds had come up from the west and hidden the sun, and the air was cold.

'What did you laugh at?'

'I don't know. We just laughed. We called it the laughing house.'

'But you must have been laughing *at* something,' she persisted. 'Did you make jokes for one another?'

'No, no, no. No jokes. Not laughing like that. Just—just silly laughing.'

'Still there must have been something to laugh at, even for silly laughing, as you call it. What sort of silly things used you laugh at?'

'What did we laugh at?' An explanation was necessary. We must have laughed at something. There must have been something that triggered it off.

'Are you not going to tell me?' Margo's face had sharpened. She stood before him, insisting on a revelation.

'Susan and I—' he mumbled.

'I know,' she said quickly. 'Susan and you in the bower. Once you got there together, you laughed your heads off. And I want to know what you laughed *at*.'

'She would make up a word—any word, any silly-sounding word—and that would set us off,' he said clutching at the first faint memory that occurred to him. 'Some silly word like—like "sligalog," or "skooka-look". That sort of thing.'

' "Skookalook". What's funny about that?'

'I don't know if that was one of them. I meant just any made-up word at all. In there, in the bower, some-how it seemed to sound—so funny.'

131

'And that's all?'

'That was all,' he said limply.

Relenting, now that he had admitted her to these privacies, she put her arm through his and rubbed her cheek against his sleeve. 'Poor Joe,' she said. 'Poor silly, simple Joe. Come on, let's go for a walk. It will soon be time to head home again.'

Later, when they got back to the car, they found Mary sitting alone in the back seat. 'What kept you two?' the child demanded in the stern voice they used to laugh at a few years ago.

'Where's Peter?' Margo asked.

'I don't know. We're not speaking,' said Mary primly. 'He has been gone for over half an hour.'

'I'll get him,' Joe volunteered. 'He won't be far away.'

'Will I go with you?'

'No. I'll be quicker alone,' said Joe. He felt that Margo knew he was glad of the opportunity to have a last look around by himself. 'Start the motor and turn on the heater,' he called back. 'There is a dew falling.'

He did not look for the boy. He walked slowly up the path to the remains of the house and walked round them once, twice, three times. He tried to move without making any sound, so that the stillness in his mind would not be disturbed. He knew he was waiting for something. But nothing came from the past—no voice, no cry, no laugh, not even the bark of a dog. He was suddenly angry. He charged down the garden and through the hedge. 'Peter!' he shouted. 'Peter! Peter!'

The echoes of his voice mocked him.

'Peter! Peter!'

Now panic gripped him. The child had had an accident! He broke into a run, crossed the lower meadow, leaped the stream and ran up the incline to the cluster of trees. 'Peter? Peter!'

Peter was so engrossed in his play that he was not aware of his father until Joe caught him by the shoulder

132

and shook him. He was on his knees at the mouth of a rabbit hole, sticking small twigs into the soft earth.

'Peter! What the hell!'

'Look, Daddy. Look! I'm donging the tower!'

'Did you not hear me shouting? Are you deaf?'

'Let me stay, Daddy. I'll have the tower donged in another five minutes.'

'Come on!' Joe dragged him away. 'Your mother will think we're both lost. Such a fright I got! Calling all over the place. Hurry up!'

'Please, Daddy, let me stay for—'

'Now, I said! It will be long past your bedtime when we get back.'

Until they got to the road, Peter had to trot to keep up with him. 'Here he is!' Joe announced. 'Playing games by himself in the wood!' Margo and Mary were listening to the radio. 'Let's get started,' said Margo. 'I'm sleepy.'

'Calling and calling, and the little blighter wouldn't even answer me!'

'Your feet are wet,' said Margo.

'That won't kill me,' said Joe gruffly.

Margo said something, but he pressed the starter and revved up the engine so that her voice was drowned.

On the way home, a sense of aloneness crept over him. Once he gave in to the temptation to glance in the mirror, but it was already dark outside, and Errigal was just part of the blackness behind them. He should never have gone back with Margo and the children. Because the past is a mirage—a soft illusion into which one steps in order to escape the present. Like hiding in the bower. How could he have told Margo that the bower had been their retreat, Susan's and his, their laughing house? The dank little den that smelled of damp and decay, which let in no sunlight and kept out no rain? Was that their retreat? And, if it came to that, how often had they laughed there? Did they not bicker and fight all the time, like Peter and Mary? 'I'll tell on you, boy. I'll tell

133

Mammy on you.' Susan's petulant voice came back to him now, clearer and harsher than the other memories.

'Go and tell then, old telltale.'

'I'm going now. I'm going now. And you'll get a beating, boy, when you come in for your tea.'

'Telltale!'

'Bully!'

How sharply he remembered: walking alone and desolate along the bottom of the meadow, imagining the stories Susan was telling their father and mother in the house, knowing that eventually he would have to go up and face the accusation and his father's hard eyes and his mother's hard mouth, how he would stammer out his side of the story and then take his beating and then be sent to bed. Was that his childhood? Why, Joe wondered, had he been so excited about the trip that morning? What had he expected to find at Corradinna—a restoration of innocence? A dream confirmed? He could not remember. All he knew now was that the visit had been a mistake. It had robbed him of a precious thing, his illusions of his past, and in their place now there was nothing—nothing at all but the truth.

'Aow! Aow! Peter nipped me! Peter nipped me!' Mary's cry shattered the sleepy quiet in the car.

'What's the matter with you?' asked Margo.

'Peter, Mammy. He nipped me in the arm! Ah, my arm! My arm!' She made no effort to control her tears.

'She kicked me first,' said Peter. 'She kicked my ankle.'

'I didn't, Mammy, I didn't. Ah-ah-ah-ah! It's bleeding! I can feel it!'

'Stop the car,' said Margo.

Joe brought the car to a stop, and Margo switched on the light. 'Now,' she said briskly. 'What happened? Show me your arm.'

'There, Mammy. Above the elbow. It's all purple.'

'There's no blood,' said Margo. 'But it is red. Why did you do that, Peter?'

'I didn't touch her until she kicked me first.'

'I was asleep, Mammy. I couldn't have kicked him.'

'Mary was asleep, Peter. Why did you nip her?'

'She's a liar!' said Peter in desperation.

The sharp smack of Margo's hand across his cheek startled them all. 'How dare you!' Margo cried. 'You know very well I do not allow you to use that word. It's a horrible thing to say about your sister! I've told you over and over again—it's a word I won't allow. I just won't have it!' She looked quickly at Joe and turned away again. 'Never let me hear you use that word again! Never!'

She had to shout her last remarks to make herself heard above the noise of Peter's howling. The crying stopped his breath, and he spluttered and choked with his face pressed against the upholstery of the seat. Mary sat timidly in the corner. Margo, uncertain what to do next, turned around facing the windscreen.

'There, now. There, there, there, son,' Joe began. 'You're all right.'

'I—I—I—' Peter stammered, breathing in.

'I know, I know, son. It's all right now. It's all over.'

He tried to catch Margo's eyes for permission to lean over and console the child. Her reluctance to look at him was sufficient. He stretched across the seat and lifted the shuddering boy in his arms and placed him gently on his knees. 'Now,' he said softly. 'That's better, isn't it? Much better. It's a good thing for a man to cry like that sometimes.'

The crying stopped, but the light body still shook when a sob took it.

'You go to sleep there on my knee, and before you know it we'll be home again. O.K.?' He switched off the light and started up the engine. The child was warm against his body. Soon the boy slept.

Silence filled the car. Through the mesmerism of motor, fleeting hedges, shadows flying from the head-lights, three words swam into Joe's head. 'Donging the

135

tower.' What did Peter mean, he wondered dreamily; what game was he playing, donging the tower? He recalled the child's face, engrossed, earnest with happiness, as he squatted on the ground by the rabbit hole. A made-up game, Joe supposed, already forgotten. He would ask him in the morning, but Peter would not know. Just out of curiosity, he would ask him, not that it mattered . . . And then a flutter of excitement stirred in him. Yes, yes, it did matter. Not the words, not the game, but the fact that he had seen his son, on the first good day of summer, busily, intently happy in solitude, donging the tower. The fact that Peter would never remember it was of no importance; it was his own possession now, his own happiness, this knowledge of a child's private joy.

Then, as he turned the car into the road that led to their house, a strange, extravagant thought struck him. He must have had moments of his own like Peter's, alone, back in Corradinna, donging his own towers. And, just as surely, his own father must have stumbled on him, and must have recognized himself in his son. And his father before that, and his father before that. Generations of fathers stretching back and back, all finding magic and sustenance in the brief, quickly destroyed happiness of their children. The past did have meaning. It was neither reality nor dreams, neither today's patchy oaks nor the great woods of his boyhood. It was simply continuance, life repeating itself and surviving.

The Saucer of Larks

They drove the first ten miles in silence. Once, at a
point where the main road veered inland and they followed a narrower track that ran along the rim of the
Atlantic, the Sergeant took his pipe from between his
teeth and said, 'This is all my kingdom as far as you can
see,' and Herr Grass said 'Yes?' in such a way that the
Sergeant was not sure if the German had understood
him. He had replied 'Yes?' to so many things that the
Sergeant had said that morning—questions about the
work they were on and other parts of the country they
had still to visit—that the old policeman resolved once
more than he would keep quiet and enjoy the sun. It
pleased him that the two in the rear seat, Guard Burke,
his assistant, and the other German, Herr Henreich, also
found conversation too difficult.

The Sergeant was a Cavan man and a garrulous man.
He had been twenty-six years in Donegal but there were
times when its beauty still shocked him; as on this spring
morning with the sea spreading out and away into the
warm sky and a high, fresh sun taking winking lights
out of the granite-covered countryside. He just had to
comment on it.

'Dammit, it's lovely, isn't it, eh? God Himself above
you and the best of creation all round you. D'you know,
only that the missus is buried away down in the mid-
lands, I wouldn't mind being laid to rest anywhere along
the coast here myself.'

'Yes?' said Herr Grass. He was young and clean and polite.

'Not that it matters a curse, I suppose, where they put you when the time comes. But it would be nice to have the sea near you and the birds above you, wouldn't it?' He stole a glance at the German's face. 'And you wouldn't be disturbed every ten minutes with funerals crawling past you—I seen them myself years ago when I was stationed in Dublin. Every ten minutes they come; everyone looking sad and miserable. I'm telling you: everything's dead in them places. Once they put you in them big cemeteries, you're finished, all right.'

'Very depressing indeed, Sergeant,' said Guard Burke from behind, hoping to match his Sergeant's mood.

'But do you see what I mean about being buried out here in the wilds?' The Sergeant was warming up. 'Out here, it's not the same at all, Burke. Out here, man, you still have life all around you. Dammit, there's so much good life around you, you haven't a chance to be really dead!'

'Very pretty. Very pretty,' said Herr Grass.

'A grand spot,' echoed Burke.

The Sergeant, who was not too sure that he had made himself clear, stuck his pipe between his teeth again.

The car went cautiously because the surface of the road was bad. Houses became fewer. Small quilts of farms lost heart in their struggle against obdurate, peaty, rocky earth and disappeared altogether. Then there was nothing but barren bogland and here and there an occasional gnarled tree, its back to the ocean, its tortuous arms outstretched to the shelter of the interior. A long, thin promontory of about three miles in length shot out at right angles to the coast line.

'That's where we're heading,' said the Sergeant. 'Out to the tip of yon neck. That's where your man's buried. Turn right when we come to the white rock below.'

'The road . . .?' began Herr Grass.

'Who would want a road out to a place like that?' said

the Sergeant. 'There's a sort of a track, as far as I remember. Drive on, man!'

They drove out along the narrow strip as far as they could but halfway the track became potted with rabbit holes. Herr Grass stopped suddenly.

'It is safer and quicker to walk, perhaps,' he said.

'Whatever you say,' said the Sergeant. 'A bit of a walk will take some of the mutton from beneath this shirt of mine.'

'Yes?' said Herr Grass.

'Just a manner of talking,' mumbled the Sergeant.

Herr Henreich, who had not spoken up to this, said something in German to Herr Grass and Herr Grass gave him the keys of the car. He then went back to the boot, opened it and took out a spade and a large white canvas bag which he folded neatly and placed under his arm. Herr Grass joined him and they talked rapidly together.

'Can I give you a hand there?' called the Sergeant.

'Yes?' said Herr Grass.

'Christ!' said the Sergeant softly to himself; then to Guard Burke, 'Come on, man, We'll lead the way.'

They followed the track which ran up the middle of the lean peninsula. At times it broadened into a road, wide enough to carry a car and then it would unexpectedly taper into a thin path and vanish into a bunker of sand.

'The man that battered out this route must never have sobered,' panted the Sergeant.

Burke was glad of the opening.

'What do you make of them?' he whispered confidentially.

'Make of what?'

'Them German fellas.'

'What do you mean, what do I make of them? They're doing a job of work here, a duty, just as they're doing the same duty all round the country. And we're here to see that everything's carried out legally and properly. That's what I make of them.' And to show Burke that he was not to be drawn into any narrow criticism of the foreigners, he turned round and shouted back to the men behind, 'Do you see the wee specks in the water away south there below the island? That's the men from Gola Island shooting their lobster pots. The lobsters are exported to France and to Switzerland and to England —aye, and to your country too. So when you go home, you can say that you seen where they come from.'

'Yes?' called Herr Grass against the wind.

'What did he say?' asked the Sergeant.

' "Yes?" ' mimicked Burke accurately.

'I'm beginning to think he says that just to annoy me,' said the Sergeant.

Half a mile from the end of the promontory, the path dipped sharply into a miniature valley, a saucer of green grass bordered by yellow sand dunes and the promontory itself ended in a high, blunt hill which broke the Atlantic wind. For a few seconds after they entered the valley, their ears still heard the rush of the breeze and they were still inclined to call to one another. Then they became aware of the silence and then, no sooner were they hushed by it, than they heard the larks, not a couple or a dozen or a score, but hundreds of them, all invisible against the blue heat of the sky, an umbrella of music over this tiny world below.

'God, isn't it grand, eh?' said the Sergeant. He dropped clumsily on the grass and screwed his face up in an effort to see the birds against the light. Guard Burke sat beside him and opened the collar of his tunic. Herr Grass and Herr Henreich stood waiting. 'Dammit, could you believe that there are places like this still in the world, eh? D'you know, there are men would give fortunes for a place like this. Fortunes. And what would they do if they got it? What would they do?'

'What, Sergeant?' asked Burke dutifully.

'They would destroy it! That's what they would do! Dig it up and flatten it out and build houses on it and ring it round with cement. Kill it. That's what they

140

would do. Kill it. Didn't I see them myself when I was stationed in Dublin years ago, making an arse of places like Malahide and Skerries and Bray. That's what I mean. Kill it! Slaughter it!'

Herr Grass had a notebook and pencil in his hand.

'This is Glennafushog?'

'Glen-na-fuiseog,' said the Sergeant, pronouncing the Gaelic name properly. 'It means the valley of the larks. You need to be careful where you walk here: you might stand on a nest and crush it. Listen to them, man! Listen to them!' He tilted his head sideways and his mouth dropped open and his big, fleshy chest rose and fell silently. Grass and Henreich and Burke looked around them casually. After a few minutes, he gathered himself together and when he spoke, he avoided Grass's face.

'Herr Grass,' he began, 'I suppose you never done an irregular thing in your life?'

'Yes?'

'What I mean is'—the old policeman sought earnestly for the right words—'I suppose you never did a wrong thing . . . did something that was against orders?'

'Disobey?'

The Sergeant did not like the word. He hesitated before accepting it. 'Aye . . . aye . . . disobey . . . that will do. Disobey. Did you ever disobey your superiors, Herr Grass?'

The German considered the question seriously. 'No . . .' he replied slowly. Then with finality, 'No.'

Burke was watching his Sergeant keenly.

'Neither did I neither,' said the Sergeant. 'Never. But there are times, I think, when it might not be such a bad thing to . . . to . . .' He saw Burke watching him and he looked away. 'There are times when a man could overlook orders . . . forget about them.'

'Overlook?' said Herr Grass.

The Sergeant got to his feet and faced the Germans.

'I'm going to ask you to do something.' His breath came in short puffs and he spoke quickly. 'Leave that

141

young lad here. Don't dig him up.'

Herr Grass stiffened.

'Let him lie here where he has all that's good in God's earth around about him. He has been here for the past eighteen years; he's part of the place by now. Leave him in it. Let him rest in peace.'

'My orders are . . .'

'Who's to know, I ask you? Who's to tell what happened? I'll fill up whatever forms you have from your government and Burke here will cause no trouble. It will be a private thing between the four of us. No one will be a bit the wiser.'

'It is getting late. We must return to Dublin today,' said Herr Grass.

'You don't understand me,' said the Sergeant. 'I'm asking you not to touch this grave—this one. Do you understand that?' He raised his voice and said each word deliberately: 'Do not touch this grave. I will not tell any one. Burke here will not tell. I will sign your papers.' He wheeled to his assistant. 'Burke, you try him. He doesn't understand me: it's the way I talk.'

'I understand,' said Herr Grass. 'But I have orders to obey.'

The four men stood awkwardly, looking at one another. The Sergeant's face which had been animated and tense while he was pleading, held its concentration until the flush of anger at Grass's refusal drained out of it. Then it went flabby and a nerve under his right eye twitched spasmodically. In the silence that followed, the heat of the sun poured down on them in waves. The air was a great void of warmth around them. Gradually the emptiness was filled again by the larks, slowly at first, then more and more of them until the saucer-valley shimmered with their singing.

The Sergeant's weighty body sagged in his uniform. He looked across the valley at the blunt hill.

'He was a young airman from Hamburg.' He spoke limply. 'And he crashed into that stump of a hill over

142

there. It was a night in the summer of '42 and his plane was burned to ashes.'

Herr Grass consulted his notebook.

'First Sergeant Werner Endler,' he read.

'He was dead when I got here. And buried. The fishermen found him about fifty yards from the plane. They made a grave and laid him to rest in it before priest or any one came because it was weather like this and the lad was badly burned.' He rubbed his hands down the legs of his trousers to dry the sweat off them.

'The exact position? Is it marked?'

'I know where it is,' said the Sergeant. 'Come on.'

He launched himself forward into the mass of heat and left the others to follow him.

The grave, a mound of grass sprinkled with wild May flowers, lay at the foot of the blunt hill. Herr Henreich opened it and put what remains he found into the white canvas bag. Then he closed the grave again and smoothed over the clay with his hands, leaving the place tidier than he had found it. While the exhumation was being done, the Sergeant paced up and down a few feet from where the Germans were working and Burke went over the dunes to relieve himself. The whole job was completed within twenty minutes.

'I think that is everything,' said Herr Grass. 'Now we are prepared.'

'Right,' said the Sergeant irritably. 'We'll go then. This bloody place is like an oven. My shirt's sticking to my back.'

On the journey back, Herr Grass was more talkative. In slow, cautious English, he told them of his early childhood, of his work in the navy during the war, of his present job with the German War Graves Commission. The following day, he said, he and Herr Henreich would motor to County Clare and on the day after that, to County Galway. Then they would bring all the remains to the special cemetry in County Wicklow where there were already over fifty Germans buried.

143

Then back to Berlin where Greta and his family of three boys were waiting for him. He showed them a photograph of Greta, a plump, carefree girl in shorts, by a lake.

Back in the police station, the Sergeant signed the papers which stated that he had witnessed the exhumation and Burke signed as witness to the Sergeant's signature. Then Herr Grass and Herr Henreich added their names and left a duplicate copy of the papers with the Sergeant. They would not stay for a meal: they had to get back to Dublin that night. They thanked the two policemen for their assistance, apologized for taking up so much of their time and departed.

'They're gone,' said Burke, looking after the car.

'Aye,' said the Sergeant.

'It's no wonder they're a powerful nation; that's what I say. Did you ever see the beat of them for efficiency? And there they are away off with a dead man in the car with them and them as happy as lambs. What do you make of them, Sergeant? And did you see that second fella, the Herr Henry bucko, did you see him digging away there as if he was digging potatoes for the dinner? Never turned a hair on his head.'

'Aye.'

'And the other lad ticking off the names in his wee book like a grocer. Aw, but they're a powerful race of people. Powerful. And then when . . .'

'Aye, powerful,' echoed the Sergeant, not knowing what he was saying. Then straightening his shoulders and pushing his stomach in with the flat of his hand, he said briskly, 'Now, Burke, back inside with us to our own duties. Have you distributed those hand bills about the dog licences?'

'This afternoon, Sergeant, I was going to do it.'

'And the tillage census in the upper parish, have you finished it yet?'

'All but three or four houses, Sergeant. I'll do them in a while of an evening on the bicycle.'

'Good,' said the Sergeant. 'That'll be that then.' The moment of efficiency died in him as quickly as it had begun. His shoulders slumped and his stomach crept out. 'I don't know a damn what came over me out there,' he said in a low voice, as if he were alone.

'What's that, Sergeant?'

'What in hell came over me? I never did the like of it in my life before. Never in all my years in the force. And then before foreigners too.' He raised his cap inches above his head, slipped his fingers under it and fumbled with his scalp. He lowered the cap again. 'I'm damned if I can understand it. The heat, maybe. The heat and the years . . . they're a treacherous combination, Burke, very treacherous.'

'What are you talking about, Sergeant?' said Burke with exaggerated innocence.

'You know bloody well what I'm talking about. And I'll tell you something here and now, Burke.' He prodded the guard's shoulder with his index finger. 'If ever a word of what happened out there at Glennafuiseog breaks your lips, to any mortal man, now or ever, as God's my judge, Burke, I'll have you sent to the wildest outpost in the country. Now, get away out with you and distribute them hand bills.'

'Very good, Sergeant.'

'And report to me again when you come back.'

'Righto, Sergeant. Righto.'

The Sergeant turned and waddled towards the building. For a man of his years and shape, he carried himself with considerable dignity.

Everything Neat and Tidy

The County Psychiatric Clinic, situated a discreet three miles beyond the town boundary, was made up of two distinct groups of buildings, as contrasting as two figures in a parable. There was the old block, originally the Mental Hospital, a granite fortress with lean, high windows and black iron doors, where the 'permanently unwell' now crooned or sobbed or fluttered away their remaining days. One hundred and fifty yards away, at the end of a dividing patch that was neither field nor lawn, there was the new block, the pride of the County Health Authority—a collection of pastel-coloured chalets with large glass doors and windows, where 'temporarily disturbed' people made model aeroplanes or lamp-shades or raffia mats with eager, brittle concentration. It was to the new block that Johnny Barr drove Mrs. MacMenamin, his mother-in-law, in his taxi every Tuesday and Thursday morning during the whole of the month of March.

At the time of Mr. Mac's death, and, indeed, for three weeks afterwards, Mrs. Mac had been wonderful. The anguish and indignity that his sudden death had let loose—the invasion by the bailiffs, the indecent haste with which the bank sold the house and the farm off to the first bidder, the shooting of the two obese, useless Labradors (who wanted two gun-shy gun dogs?), getting Sarah, the old housekeeper, accepted in the Old People's Home run by the Nazareth nuns, and only after much pleading—all this she had borne so quietly and so courageously that Johnny realized he had never known her before. Previously, he had thought of her as a vague, diffident, impractical woman. Now he admired her. So that when her son, Henry, who was a doctor, ignored her requests to go and live with him in his flat in Dublin, Johnny promptly offered her the spare room in his neat terrace house with his wife, Mary, and himself. She accepted, and he was glad to have her. It never occurred to him that this would strike her as the final, crushing indignity.

For three weeks, she behaved as if nothing in her life had changed. She read in her bedroom, or did a little light housework, or sometimes just sat in the tiny, precise parlour and gazed out placidly at the children playing in the street after school. Then, one Sunday after supper, when Johnny and Mary were worrying over the problem of whether they should go ahead and buy a second taxi, Mrs. MacMenamin began to cry quietly. Johnny was the first to notice her tears.

'It's O.K., Mrs. Mac,' he said. He winked at her. 'Even if a second cab leaves us short for a while, we won't put you out to work!'

Before he had finished speaking, she began to moan. Her moaning grew into a wail, and the wail thinned and rose to a shriek, and when they held her, Johhny by the right arm and Mary by the left, she flung back her head and screamed and screamed at the ceiling. The paroxysm lasted less than a minute. When her struggling was strongest and her distraught cries broke against the walls of the confining room, she suddenly went limp. They carried her long, awkward body upstairs and laid her on the bed, and tiptoed down again and talked in whispers. Later, the doctor called and said, 'Reaction . . . nerves . . . temporary . . .' and arranged for an appointment for her at the County Psychiatric Clinic. The clinic advised electric-shock treatments—two times a week, nine treatments in all—and Johnny took on the job of driving her

147

there and back, because there was no one else to do it, and because ever since that Sunday night, seeing her so helpless and so pale and so exposed on top of the bed-clothes, his admiration for her had turned into affection.

Johnny came to enjoy those trips to the clinic. Occasionally he calculated that they were costing him a lot of money (in wear and tear on the car, not to talk of lost fares), but it was pleasant to get away from the smelly taxi rank and out into the spring air of the country. While he waited for Mrs. Mac, he walked around the grounds, admiring the trim paths and the careful gardens and the tidy shrubs and thinking how lucky he was—a wife who loved and respected him (and who had now become so thrifty that her watchfulness sometimes annoyed him), a compact, comfortable home, a business that was expanding. Every morning, too, he stood and gazed for a short time across the patch of land that was neither field nor lawn, and then, for some reason, his thoughts invariably went back to the time before he was married, when he went out to the MacMenamin's farm every Sunday afternoon to take Mary for a drive. But most of the waiting time he spent strolling around the chalets, which, to all outward appearances, might have been a collection of summer holiday houses.

After four or five visits, Johnny was convinced that the electric-shock treatments were a failure. The only effect they had on Mrs. Mac—and he did not mention this to Mary, because it lasted for only about twenty minutes after the old woman came out of the sky-blue chalet—was to make her arrogant and overbearing, even more imperious then Lady Hartnell of Killard, whom he drove to the bank once a month. Mrs. Mac would march up to the taxi and climb into the back seat and say, 'Off you go, John!' as if he were her private chauffeur. Of course, the treatments temporarily impaired her memory—the doctor had told him to expect that—and as he drove her home he protected himself against her bumptiousness by encouraging her confusion. It was harmless enough fun, Johnny asking her how things were on the farm these days and she replying that Mr. Mac had just bought a huge combine harvester, or the latest milking machine, or a very expensive pedigree bull. Or Johnny would wonder out loud how the spring sowing was going, and she would list off such a series of crops as the biggest farm in the whole of Ireland could never have produced. The grander she got with him, the more he chuckled to himself. But by the time he drew up at the door, her affectations all vanished and her memory came back, and she was a silent, timid, fearful, ageing woman again. He helped her out of his taxi and guided her tenderly into the house and handed her over to his wife as gently as if she were a baby, because then, seeing her so reduced, and remembering her as she had once been, he regretted his baiting and resolved never to mention the farm again.

The MacMenamins never had the wealth or the position of Lady Hartnell of Killard. But they might have, had Mr. Mac not drunk so heavily, had Mrs. Mac been more practical, had they kept Henry on the farm (and it was one of the best farms in County Tyrone) instead of making a doctor of him, had the rich land been worked and not let to neighbours. They lived imprudently, carelessly, without thought for the future. When he recalled those Sunday afternoons, Johnny remembered the feeling of annoyance that had pricked him every time he saw electric lights burning all over the house in broad daylight, the apples rotting in barrels in the pantry, the wrought-iron gates hanging from one hinge, or the buckets rusting in the water troughs. Every time he went there, he wanted to throw off his coat and fix fences, paint doors, and gather up fallen branches for firewood. So much waste. Such great indifference. He would knock at the door; no one would answer, and he would go into the high, panelled hall. Mr. Mac would be in a deep sleep before a dead fire in the drawing room, or puzzling futilely over pages of figures and accounts.

149

Mrs. Mac would be upstairs, reading in one of the bedrooms, or crocheting in the breakfast room. Sarah, the old housekeeper, would be dozing in the kitchen, although the table would be piled high with the lunch dishes. Even Mary, who knew to expect him, was seldom waiting for him. He would find her in the fields, wandering around in search of hens' nests, or down in one of the byres playing with a litter of young pups. The whole setup confused and annoyed him, and yet fascinated him. When he was with them, he was conscious only of impatience. What a business he would have made of that place! How he could have run it! Yet when he went home to his own house in the town—before he married, he lived in three rooms as natty and precise as a doll's house, above the bakery where his father was night watchman—he forgot the chaos and the decay and remembered only the tranquillity of their lives. He would look at his mother, birdlike, shrivelled, sharp with the lifelong battle against poverty, and think of Mrs. Mac, who had floated serenely above hardship. He would watch his father roll cigarettes (by making his own, he saved three-pence a packet) and remember the carpet at Mrs. Mac's feet ruined by cigar burns. The contrast between the life he had been reared to and the life he now tasted made him dissatisfied with both. It would have taken so little, he knew, to win him over to the MacMenamins. If Mr. Mac had said even once to him, 'You're early today,' or 'We thought you were never coming,' or if Mrs. Mac had asked him even once what his job was or what his ambitions were, then there would have been no conflict. But they gave him as little of their attention as they gave to one another, or to the land, or to the fat, wheezing Labradors, who wandered unheeded upstairs and downstairs. And still, those Sunday afternoon visits were the highlight of his week. It was not for Mary alone that he spread his trousers under the mattress every Saturday night so that they would have a sharp crease, and bathed himself in the iron tub in the miniature scullery, and polished his shoes until they glistened. It was primarily for her, of course; but it was also for Mrs. Mac, and even for Mr. Mac, and, in some vague way that he could not understand himself, out of deference to the ramshackle farm itself.

In the last week of Mrs. Mac's course of treatments, Mary came across the notice of Sarah's death in the Home. Johnny agreed that the news must be kept from Mrs. Mac. If she was making progress—and there was little evidence that she was—this would set her back. Yet when she came out of the clinic later that morning and said to him, 'Hurry up! I have shopping to do! Don't sit there leering at me!' he knew he was going to tell her.

He waited until they had passed through the gates. Then he said, 'How do you feel today, Mrs. Mac?'

'Quite well, thank you, John.' She looked very alert that day, much better than after any of the previous treatments.

'One more visit and you're finished up, Mrs. Mac.'

'I know.'

'What will you do with yourself then?'

'I haven't decided yet. Travel, maybe. Go to London for a few weeks. D'you know, I haven't been in London since Henry qualified.' Her eyes became troubled. 'But travel is so expensive, isn't it?' she went on. 'It takes so much money, doesn't it?'

'As well as that, you couldn't very well leave the farm at this time of year,' he prompted.

'Yes,' she said, but so dreamily that he knew she was agreeing with her own private thoughts.

'This is your busiest time on the land, isn't it, Mrs. Mac? This is the time all you farmers work a sixteen-hour day, isn't it?'

'Yes,' she said in the same vague way. 'Quite right . . . yes . . .'

He watched her in the mirror to see the brows furrow in concentration and the lips fumble with one another, as they always did on these trips home. But not today.

151

There was going to be no harmless fun today. An uneasiness stirred in him. 'I suppose you heard about Sarah, Mrs. Mac?'

'Sarah? Who's Sarah?'

'Sarah, the old housekeeper. You remember Sarah, don't you? Always giving backchat to you!'

'I . . . yes, I think I remember her.'

'I knew you would.'

He paused, conscious of cruelty. But before he could muster charity he heard himself saying, 'She died last night.'

'Sarah? My housekeeper?'

'Funeral tomorrow after last Mass.'

'Sarah?' she whispered.

'Dead,' he said.

'Ooh, God!' She did not cry, but she moaned. She gripped her elbow and rocked herself backwards and forwards and groaned in a high monotone that terrified him. He thought of stopping the taxi, of getting her a drink of brandy, of rushing her to a doctor, but then decided instead to get her home as quickly as possible.

By the time they reached the house, she had quietened. He put his arm around her and supported her into the hallway, where Mary met them.

'Quick!' he snapped. 'Get her bed ready!'

Mary stared stupidly at them.

'For God's sake, move!' he roared, because he was afraid that Mrs. Mac would collapse in his arms. 'Move! Move! Move!'

He lifted her off the ground—she was as light as a child—and carried her upstairs as tenderly and as lovingly as if she were a baby. Afterwards, when she was asleep and he was having a meal, Mary kissed him on the forehead and said, 'Thank you, Johnny. You've been better to her than any son could have been.' He did not answer, because he was angry with himself, because he felt guilty, and because he was frightened. There had been a moment in the taxi, after Mrs. Mac did not respond to his first prompting about the farm, when a strange loneliness had touched him; what frightened him was that that loneliness, that isolation, might touch him again, might even enter into him.

The following Thursday was Mrs. Mac's last visit. It was a glorious spring morning that was both urgent and still. The sun was high, and the air was clean and clear, and the grounds had never looked fresher nor more attractive. He walked round the paths and looked at the flowers he had seen push into life, and strolled between the neat, trimmed shrubs. It was a morning for alertness, a morning when a man can look back over the past and take pride in his achievements, and look forward to the future and plan confidently for it. But somehow Johnny was conscious only of wistfulness. There was growth and vitality around him and beneath him, but his senses were muted with a vague nostalgia. He left the new block and gazed across the patch that was neither field nor lawn. And then, for the first time, he understood the clinic's special attraction for him. It could have been a part of the farm. This discovery, and the start of recognition that accompanied it, gave him a moment's pleasure, a delight that vanished as soon as it was felt. It gave way to a quick, flooding panic. To hell with the farm, he thought, angrily marching back to the new block! To hell with it! To hell with it!

Mrs. Mac found him in the waiting room, reading magazines. He jumped to his feet when he saw her.

'All set?' he said.

'At long last. Let's get home quickly, Johnny. I never want to see this place again.' And she giggled nervously, because she thought that a nurse who was passing might have heard her.

They got into the taxi. For the first time, she sat beside him in the front. He waited for 'Off you go, John!' but it did not come. As they passed through the gates, he took a quick look back at the grounds and the two groups of buildings. They looked chaste and festive in the sunlight.

Mrs. Mac smiled happily at the road ahead. 'Someday, Johnny, I'll have to repay you for all these trips. You have been more than kind to me.'

'There's only one way you can repay me, Mrs. Mac,' he said, laughing unnaturally.

'What way is that?'

'Leave me the farm when you die.'

'There's no one deserves it more,' she said.

Johnny remained silent, frowning to himself. Mrs. Mac seemed much better today; she was almost complacent. For some reason he did not understand, each improvement in her health seemed to add to a growing melancholy inside himself. Now he tried to take heart from the ambiguity of her last reply. So she really thought she still owned the farm, did she?

'Is this—is this Wednesday, Johnny?' Mrs. Mac said.

'Thursday,' he said.

'Then I'm a day late.'

'Late for what, Mrs. Mac?'

'For the funeral—Sarah's funeral.'

'Sarah was buried a week ago, Mrs. Mac. You're not a day late—you're eight days late!'

'Eight days? How—where—where did the time go?'

'How should I know?' he snapped. Then, persuasively, he added, 'I was at the funeral.'

'Oh, you were? That's good. I'm glad we were represented.'

'No one there but myself. The only mourner.'

'Poor Sarah,' she said, dismissing her with a sigh. 'May God have mercy on her.'

'Remember how she used to sleep in front of the fire, Mrs. Mac? Remember? She would pile up the dishes and pull up a comfortable chair and spread herself out and—'

'She was so stupid,' said Mrs. Mac briskly. 'At least half a dozen times I taught her how to make pastry. But she never could learn. She really was a peasant, Sarah.'

154

'Pastry?' he said, pouncing on the scrap of new information.

'And so lazy! Heavens, how I stood her for so long! But let's think of pleasant things, shall we? D'you know, Johnny, it'll be summer before we know it.' She smiled serenely out at the countryside. 'I wonder what Mary'll have for lunch today,' she said interestedly.

Mary was waiting for them at the door, dancing with excitement; Henry was coming from Dublin that evening to take Mrs. Mac back with him. There had been a letter in the midday delivery, and on its heels a telegram with the same news. He had forgotten he had written! So typical of Henry!

Mrs. Mac took the news as calmly as if she had expected it. 'Henry was always a good boy,' she said to Mary. 'But I love your Johnny every bit as dearly now. He has been as good to me as any son.' She went upstairs to pack.

Johnny pretended that he had a run to do. He dashed out of his house, sprang into his taxi, and drove recklessly towards the centre of the town. He steered wildly, in full stampede, and through the windscreen he saw only the farm as he had known it in all its autumn decay and beauty. Mrs. Mac had escaped. She was at peace, no longer frightened by the past and the morass of memory, but her release had deprived him forever of the farm and the Sunday afternoons and all the tidy, attainable ambitions of his single days. Chilled by this sudden personal disaster, he drove faster and faster, as if he could escape the moment when he would take up the lonely burden of recollections that the dead had fled from and the living had forgotten.